THE LAST WAY STATION

D0121629

THE LAST WAY STATION

KENT CONWELL

WHEELER
CHIVERS

This Large Print edition is published by Wheeler Publishing, Waterville, Maine, USA, and by BBC Audiobooks Ltd, Bath, England.
Wheeler Publishing is an imprint of The Gale Group.
Wheeler is a trademark and used herein under license.
Copyright © 2007 by Kent Conwell.
The moral right of the author has been asserted.

LIBRARY OF CONGRESS CATALOGING-IN-PUBLICATION DATA

Conwell, Kent.
    The last way station / by Kent Conwell.
      p. cm. — (Wheeler Publishing large print Western)
    ISBN-13: 978-1-59722-645-5 (softcover : alk. paper)
    ISBN-10: 1-59722-645-9 (softcover : alk. paper)
    1. Large type books. I. Title.
PS3553.O547L37 2007
813'.54—dc22   2007030040

BRITISH LIBRARY CATALOGUING-IN-PUBLICATION DATA AVAILABLE

Published in 2007 in the U.S. by arrangement with Leisure Books, a division of Dorchester Publishing Co., Inc.
Published in 2008 in the U.K. by arrangement with Dorchester Publishing Co., Inc.

U.K. Hardcover: 978 1 405 64312 2 (Chivers Large Print)
U.K. Softcover: 978 1 405 64313 9 (Camden Large Print)

Printed in the United States of America on permanent paper
10 9 8 7 6 5 4 3 2 1

THE LAST WAY STATION

THE LAST WAY STATION

"Dammit to hell, Jake, you best listen to me. I don't like this job. I swear we're both loco, you for dumping your last two-bits in a crazy pipe dream that ain't got no chance of ever seein' daylight, an' me for leaving Arizona to tag after you."

Three-Fingers Bent popped a pebble from under his bay's front left shoe and looked up at his young sidekick. He shifted his chaw of tobacco from one cheek to the other and nodded to the lush valley below. "Them folks down there in that Mormon town scare me worse'n a starvin' grizzly." The old man dropped the horse's hoof. "From what I hear, Mormons would as soon string a feller up as pray for him, 'specially uninvited cowpokes like us." He loosed an arc of tobacco to punctuate his words as he climbed back in the saddle.

Jake Slade shifted around in his double-cinched Texas saddle and hooked a leg around the saddle horn. He rested his gnarled hand on the walnut grip of the .44 on his hip and gazed across the broad valley, his sun-browned skin stretching taut across his broad cheekbones.

A wide, shining river, the Canadian, meandered through the middle of the broad basin, bisecting luxuriant fields of new winter wheat and late season sorghum. Afternoon shadows gathered about a neat village in the horseshoe bend of the river.

Slade didn't like the job either. He, too, had heard the stories about the Mormons, about the massacre at Mountain Meadows, but he'd never run across any jasper who had firsthand knowledge of the deed. He wasn't certain if they were just stories, rumors, or the truth. Regardless, he was going to watch his step.

Slade removed his slouch hat and ran his fingers through short-cropped hair. The Nez Perce in his gray eyes narrowed with suspicion, but the white man in his heart hoped Bent was wrong.

By hitching up with his boss, Bill Harnden, in this venture, the young half-breed had invested every last penny of his savings and dreams in a stage run from Fort Atkinson, Arkansas to El Paso, Texas, hoping to cash in on the new business and buy a ranch on the Mogollon Plateau in Arizona Territory.

And now, here in a small settlement in the middle of the Texas Panhandle, Slade was ready to tie both ends of the stage run together. Within hours, either his dream would come true or five years' dreaming, sacrifice, and work would vanish like a rolling tumbleweed.

Bent snorted. "You hear what I said?"

The younger man turned his gray eyes on Bent. "We haven't even met these folks yet. Don't you reckon you just might be jumping to conclusions?"

The old man shook his head emphatically. "It don't take no conclusion for me to remember it was them Mormons what *massacred* all them settlers up in Utah country ten-twelve years back — a hundred and forty of them poor folks slaughtered like hogs — men, women, and children." He snorted again and shook his head at the sprawling community below. "You know Mormons don't cotton to outsiders. They want to be by theirselves. What guarantee you got that them down there won't do the same to us as them others?"

With a faint grin on his weather-browned face, Slade studied his old friend. Over their years together on Bill Harnden's stage line, the young half-breed had come to realize that Bent was one to ride the river with. Though the old man was cantankerous and sometimes hotheaded, Slade had never taken his partner's fears lightly. He shook his head. "Nothing's guaranteed, Bent." He hooked a thumb across the valley. "That's why Nana's with us."

Bent looked in the direction Slade indicated. On the far rim, a dark figure sat motionless on a small pony. The figure was Nana, Slade's Apache brother.

Although Bent had fought Apaches ever since he was a button, over the past few years he had reached an understanding with Nana. He admired the young warrior's courage as much as his devotion to Slade, "Busca," as the Apaches called him; but of course, the old man would never admit having any such human feelings as admiration for an Apache. He groused. "One set of extra eyes ain't much of a comfort."

Slade pulled his hat down on his forehead. He squinted over his shoulder into the setting sun. That drifter back on the Staked Plains still nagged at him. "Maybe not, but if I had my choice of any pair of eyes, it would be Nana's."

"All I can say," Bent added, scratching his grizzled jaw. "Is that old Bill shoulda sent a couple gunnies with us. I sure as shooting wouldn't have complained about that at all."

Slade's smile broadened into a grin, splitting his dark face like a new moon. "Now, Bent. You not complain? I reckon that's kinda hard for me to picture. Why, you know yourself you got a natural, God-given talent for finding something to fuss over," he said. "And if you can't find a reason, you usually make one up."

Bent stared at Slade, trying to maintain the frown on his craggy face, but the infectious smile on the young half-breed's face broke through his resolution. He snorted and jerked his bay around. "Go to hell," he said gruffly, kicking his heels into his dun's flanks and sending the animal skittering down the slope into the darkening valley.

Slade laughed and followed.

Across the valley, Nana disappeared into a grove of cottonwoods.

As they approached the small village, Bent muttered. "Women being what they is, how do you reckon these old boys put up with more than one wife?"

CHAPTER TWO

In the blacksmith shop, Joseph Ware paused to squint into the setting sun at the two figures approaching on horseback. He laid his three-pound cross peen hammer on the anvil and brushed the layer of coal dust off his muscular forearms. Travelers were uncommon to New Gideon since the village lay far off the western trails. He glanced over his shoulder at his wife who had come to stand in the doorway of the neat frame house next to his shop. "We will have guests tonight, Rebecca."

Dutifully, the plump little woman nodded and disappeared inside.

Open and friendly, Joseph held up his hand in greeting as Slade and Bent drew up at the water trough in front of the shop. "Welcome, strangers. My name's Joseph Ware. It'll be night soon. If you're not in a hurry, we'd be right pleased for you to take supper with us."

Slade stood in the stirrups and grinned to himself. The town blacksmith. Maybe luck was on their side. They had stumbled across the very man they had hoped to find. "That's right hospitable, Mr. Ware. This here is my partner, Three-Fingers Bent, and I'm Jake Slade."

The blacksmith studied the two riders a moment. Both wore cowpoke duds, heavy denims, and loose-fitting homespun shirts. But a frown creased his forehead when he saw that the younger one wore a deerskin vest and what looked like Indian-made moccasins. And riding on the young man's left hip was an Indian war club. Beneath one fender of the saddle was an elmwood bow in a deerskin case with two-dozen iron-pointed arrows. Under the other fender was a matching deerskin case sheathing a battered Winchester. The only weapon Ware did not see was the coiled slingshot in Slade's vest pocket. He nodded over his shoulder. "Stable's out back."

Joseph Ware watched the two men dismount. The younger one moved with the grace of a mountain lion. He was slender, but Ware had the feeling that the young man was tough as the iron he tempered in his shop and twice as durable.

■ ■ ■ ■

Later, Joseph Ware leaned back from the table and patted his stomach. "Fine meal, Rebecca. I hope our guests enjoyed it," he said, looking at Bent who was still putting himself around a thick slab of dried apple pie after inhaling succulent roasted beef, boiled corn, pungent steamed cabbage, and mouth-watering home-baked bread.

"Best I've had in months, Mrs. Ware," Slade said, turning his gray eyes back to the blacksmith, awaiting his host's answer to Slade's proposition.

He had quickly recognized that Ware was a fair man, and as such, his decision could prove invaluable. If Ware refused to go along with their plan to set up the final relay station here in New Gideon, then Slade was without a spokesman.

That meant he would be forced to approach the village on his own, which, he told himself, could prove to be as slippery a job as sprinkling salt on the five-inch stump of a bobcat. If Joseph Ware could see the value in Slade's idea, then at least the young half-breed had one vote on his side.

Bent ignored Slade and Ware, determined to wreak as much damage to the substantial meal before him as he could, although he warily eyed the glass of milk by his plate. He hadn't tasted milk in forty years, but that was the only drink on the table, and Western manners dictated that guests never refuse freely-offered grub.

Still wondering about Ware's other wives, Bent flashed a gap-toothed grin at Mrs. Ware who sat across the table. She was a plain woman dressed in calico, but she gave the impression of being right sturdy, the kind of pioneer woman who could rustle up solid grub from next to nothing; could whip out a Sunday-go-to-meeting dress from a couple flour sacks; and could make a soddy look like a castle. "Mighty filling grub, ma'am," he said. "Reckon I can't remember when I had tastier dried apple pie."

Mrs. Ware ducked her head, uncomfortable with praise. "I'm grateful it pleasures you so much, Mr. Bent. We have plenty." She shoved the tin pie plate across the table, pleased to see any man or boy pack himself from her table.

"It's better with a big swallow of milk, Mr. Bent," said Joseph.

Reluctantly, Bent sipped the milk. The liquid was passable, but nothing could take the place of hot coffee, black as midnight and strong as an unbathed cowboy.

The burly blacksmith chuckled when he spotted the grimace on Bent's face when the old man sipped the milk. "Reckon our ways are some different than yours, Mr. Bent. Hot drinks are forbidden us, as are alcohol and tobacco."

Grateful he had the foresight to spit out his chaw of tobacco before entering the house, Bent reached for the pie. "Well, folks is different. Me, I reckon I can get by without the coffee as long as I got this pie," he said, cutting a slab twice as wide as the first.

Mrs. Ware beamed. "More cream, Mr. Bent?"

He held his plate for her. With a long-handled wooden spoon, she skimmed a thick layer of rich, yellow cream from a jar of milk and plopped it on top of the steaming slab of pie.

Joseph Ware cleared his throat. "Well, Mr. Slade. Concerning your proposition, I figure you're heading for more trouble than if you'd brought in a plague of locusts at harvest time. Folks here don't much cotton to new faces but what they be of our faith. And the fact that we've been having trouble with rustlers the last five or six years don't help none."

"I understand, Mr. Ware. We don't want

to change anything around here, but we are interested in changing things out west. You see, in Utah last year, at a place called Promontory Point, the railroads from the east and west connected. This country of ours is building itself a big spiderweb of trails so people can spread over this land and take advantage of all it has to offer."

"That's my point, Mr. Slade. We don't want newcomers here."

Slade rested his elbows on the table and leaned forward, his eyes holding Joseph Ware's. "Call me Jake. And we don't want newcomers here either. We want them out in Arizona Territory — maybe some across the Staked Plains in West Texas or New Mexico Territory."

He paused to clear his throat. "But if it'll make you rest easier, Mr. Ware, I'm on your side. I don't agree with my boss about a station in New Gideon, and I've got two good reasons."

The big blacksmith frowned.

Slade continued. "I got my life savings invested in this stage line, and I don't think any line should run through any town that doesn't want it. If we go where we're not wanted, I figure we'll have trouble sooner or later."

Ware grunted. "Then why did you come

to New Gideon in the first place?"

"Fair question. To be honest, it's the shortest way. Drew a straight line from El Paso to Fort Atkinson, Arkansas, and that line cut right through your valley. We can save a day or so of stage travel by that route." Slade paused, then added wryly, "If you ever done much stage riding, Mr. Ware, you know how pleasurable it is to save a couple days."

Ware laughed, a broad, rollicking bellow. "I've ridden enough of them bouncing seats to appreciate what you're saying, Jake. But you said you had two reasons. What's the other, if you don't mind me nosing about?" The blacksmith leaned forward, resting his muscular forearms on the kitchen table.

Slade shrugged. "I just told you. If we go where we're not wanted, sooner or later, we got trouble. This country's wide open. I figure it would go a heap easier for us if we set up a relay station back north. Country's a heap more rugged, which means it would take more time, but we wouldn't have no one to worry over except for the two old boys running the station."

"Then why do it? I mean, come here to New Gideon."

A wry grin tugged at the somber half-breed's lips as he leaned forward. "Bill

Harnden's a family man. He figured any community could use the cash business, and it will save a little time, like I said."

Ware leaned back and folded his arms across his broad chest. "Your boss sounds like a good man."

"He is." Slade glanced down at his large hands that were spread out fanlike on the handcrafted cottonwood table. His knuckles were large knobs, scarred from years of fighting with every drunken cowpoke or wet-eared button who figured to stomp him into the ground because he was a half-breed.

He had learned to take care of himself with his fists as well as with his brain. Long before Slade left the Mimbre Apaches to scout for J. E. B. Stuart, the old chief, Mangas Coloradas, took him aside and laid a wrinkled finger on Slade's forehead. "Great warriors fight the battles here first." The young man understood. Two months later, the Blue Coats murdered Magnas Coloradas. Slade would never forget the treachery.

Now, Slade hoped he had fought this first battle wisely. He cleared his throat and said. "Of course, Mr. Ware, we can go around if you folks want us to. But even if we do, we'll still be neighbors. Bill just figured that you'd want first shot at a business that would bring fresh cash into your community."

Ware rocked forward in his chair and frowned.

Slade added. "You give us a right-of-way through your valley, and we'll put in a relay station here for your people to operate. That means we'd be buying extra feed for the stock, grub for the passengers, and hire on three or four of your people as wranglers to handle the stock. New Gideon will pick up a right nice bundle of extra cash. Why, you as the local blacksmith will have a ready-made passel of work at your back door just taking care of the stock. You might even build yourself a larger blacksmith shop."

Ware remained silent, studying Slade. The young man made sense. Keep the relay station in New Gideon among their own people. That way, no outsiders could come in. And there would be no neighbors.

Finally, he said. "Blacksmith, huh? That's why you came straight to me."

Slade shrugged and gave him a sheepish grin. "Be kinda foolish not to, don't you think?"

Ware grinned. "We're simple people here. We don't need much. But I see your point. Every community can use an extra cash business."

Slade shot Bent a satisfied grin before turning back to the blacksmith. "Where do we go from here?"

"Tomorrow," said Ware, rising to his feet. "Tomorrow I'll take you to the Stake High Council."

The wiry young man frowned.

Ware explained. "That's our governing body. All decisions affecting the Stake" — he made a sweeping gesture — "this community, are made there." A regulator clock on the mantel chimed nine o'clock. Ware nodded to his wife who had just finished cleaning the kitchen. She scurried into another room, the bedroom, Slade guessed. Ware hooked his thumb to an adjoining room. "Your beds are ready. You must excuse us. We rise at four."

Slade stopped him. "What do you think the council will do, Mr. Ware?"

"Call me Joseph."

Slade nodded.

Ware continued, a frown knitting his forehead. "There are many who are against changing the old ways. What will they do, you ask? Who knows? I like your idea, Jake, but don't get your hopes up too high."

Later in the dark, Bent read Slade's mind. "What do you think, Jake? Still worried about that grubliner we run across back on the Staked Plains?"

Slade rolled over on his bunk and stared into the darkness where Bent lay. He was uncomfortable sleeping under a roof. "I don't figure we'll see him again, but I'm still spooky about the way he walked in with the three of us around the fire. It surprised him. Two white men and an Apache. That don't mix."

Bent laughed away his young partner's concern. "At least, it wasn't Jack Barker."

Slade grunted with relief as he remembered the lawman who had tracked him for over three years until learning that all the murder charges against Slade had been dismissed. "That's over and done with."

"I know, but I forget every once in a while. He sure hung after you for a long time. Like a bulldog."

"That kinda money riding on a man's head, wouldn't you?"

Bent paused. "Considering the size of the reward, I reckon so."

Slade said nothing.

"These folks seem to be right nice, but I sure could use a cup of coffee. Somehow, it don't seem Christian not to serve coffee at a meal."

"Reckon not everybody guzzles it like you do, Bent."

Bent replied defensively. "I don't guzzle, but I do cotton to it. Why do you reckon they don't?"

"Can't say. Maybe that's somehow part of the way they believe."

"Maybe so, but it sure is odd."

"Most of us is odd in one way or another."

"Maybe." He paused, then muttered. "Wonder where his extra wives be?"

Slade grunted.

After a few moments of silence, Bent asked. "What do you figure is goin' to happen tomorrow? About the right-of-way, I mean."

"I don't feel too good about it. But, I just want to settle it fast. If they don't want it, fine. We'll find another spot and be done with it. I'm ready to hightail it out of Texas for Tucson."

Bent grunted. "Old Bill will send word if your sister and her husband come in early."

The young half-breed rolled over and stared into the darkness above him. The crisscrossed ropes that supported the blanket on which he lay cut into his back. "I reckon you're right, but that's not as good as being there should they come in."

Bent didn't reply. For several minutes, the two men lay without moving. Then a soft snore sounded from Bent's bed. Slade grinned and closed his own eyes, but sleep eluded him.

The ticktock marking the swing of the pendulum on the regulator clock kept up a steady beat. Finally the clock chimed ten. Slade was still awake. He slipped from bed and into his moccasins and eased out of the room. He'd throw his blanket under one of the cottonwoods by the river.

There was no moon, but the stars bathed the valley with a cool, blue glow. The broad sweep of the Canadian River hissed and bubbled as it rushed past the shore and tumbled over sunken logs. Slade inhaled the fresh air and spread his blanket by an ancient cottonwood.

Moments after he lay down, distant voices reached his ears. He listened. The voices grew louder. Slade sat up and pulled himself into the shadows surrounding the massive trunk of the cottonwood.

Downriver, two figures, one large, one small, emerged from the darkness. Their voices were angry.

The shadowy figures halted on the far side of the cottonwood. The smaller one, a woman, spoke sharply. "It's the same problem, Garth. You're afraid of your father, and you'll always be afraid of your father."

Uncomfortable at being forced to eavesdrop, Slade eased to his feet and pressed against the tree trunk as Garth Smith replied, his words tight with suppressed anger. "You know better than that, Sarah. I am not afraid. I respect him. That is how we believe. If you'd go to the meetings instead of wandering up and down this river all the time, you'd know that."

"Don't start up with that again, Garth Smith. I don't fit in here at New Gideon. I feel like I'm being shunned."

Garth grunted. "We don't shun, Sarah. You know that."

Her voice tightened in anger. "Well, that's how everyone treats me. Even you when your father's around. I just wish I had the money to leave this horrible place and the cruel people. You know I don't go to the meetings because I can't believe like you, and I won't be a hypocrite like some."

"Don't say that. We're not hypocrites. The rules our church gives us are for our own benefit. Can't you get that through your thick head?"

Sarah snapped back. "It might be thick, but I don't wear a pious face to meeting and then play the high and mighty when I'm in public. I don't know what you call it, but I call it hypocrisy. And I won't lick anyone's boots like you do. I —"

A sharp pop cut through the night. Sarah gasped in shock at the slap.

The man hissed. "I told you not to speak to me like that. Women have their place here. Next time, I'll really —"

Slade stepped from behind the cottonwood and spun the young man around. His gnarled fist cut off the man's words in midsentence as hard knuckles loosened a few teeth. Garth went sliding across the sandy shore on his back.

CHAPTER THREE

Sarah spun in alarm at the shadowy figure that had suddenly appeared out of nowhere. She pressed her hands to her lips.

"If you want to keep on breathing, youngster," Slade growled at the downed man, "don't slap a woman when I'm around. You got to slap someone, slap a man."

Garth shook his head, clearing the cobwebs. He stared up at the strange man standing over him. With a grunt of anger, he pushed himself to his feet and, swinging wildly, rushed Slade.

Slade stepped to his right at the last moment as a roundhouse right whistled by his ear. He threw a straight right into the man's jaw. Garth spun, but remained on his feet, shaking his head.

Stepping back, Slade dropped his hands to his side and eyed the stunned man. "Smartest thing you can do, boy, is back away. I'd hate to make the lady think any less of you."

His words were like pouring coal oil on a fire. With a wild cry, Garth rushed in again, this time swerving to his left where Slade had dodged before. Slade stepped to the other side this time and looped a left down which caught Garth on his right cheekbone, splitting it open. Blood, dark in the starlight, poured down his cheek.

Stunned, the young man, his breath coming in gasps, touched his cheek. He stared at the blood on his fingers, astonished.

"Were I you, I'd apologize to the lady, and then get myself back home to Mama." But Slade knew the young man would not heed his words. The young man had been embarrassed in front of the girl. He couldn't back away now so Slade would have to end it as quickly as possible. No sense in the boy taking too much of a beating even though he did deserve one for slapping the girl around.

With a growl of anger, Garth spun on Slade. When he did, he dropped his guard, and Slade, pivoting on his left foot and following through with his whole body, slammed his fist into the boy's jutting jaw. Like an empty flour sack, the boy sagged to the ground.

Slade glanced at the girl whose face was hidden in shadows. "You all right, miss?"

"Who — who are you?"

Slade told her, then nodded at the inert figure on the ground at their feet. "I didn't mean to eavesdrop, but you two walked right up on my soogan." He nodded to the blanket spread beneath the cottonwood and then back at the man on the ground. "You want me to help you get him wherever he belongs?"

She shook her head. "No. No, I can. I . . ." Her words trailed off. "Please — please, leave us alone."

The girl was scared. No sense in frightening her any more, but Slade felt strangely drawn to her. She was gutsy, no doubt about that. He dipped his head and stepped back as she knelt and helped the young boy to his feet.

"A hell of a way to begin asking these folks for help," Slade muttered softly. But he knew he would do the same thing again if he saw a man mistreat a woman. After all, the girl appeared only a year or two younger than his own sister for whom he had searched for fourteen years before finding.

Minutes later, Slade found a grassy bower in the middle of a plum thicket. If any righteous citizens decided to look him up later on that night, they'd have to be mighty slick to reach him without awakening him.

■ ■ ■ ■

Next morning, Slade and Bent sat at a table loaded down with solid, rib-sticking grub. Steam rose from a platter of thick beefsteaks and a bowl of cream gravy flecked with black pepper. The rich mellowness of freshly baked bread, the golden bouquet of Mormon johnnycakes, and the spicy perfume of dried apple pie filled the room with succulent, mouth-watering aromas. Mrs. Ware set a pitcher of cold milk on the table.

"Help yourself, gentlemen," said the blacksmith, pouring the milk and setting the glasses before the two men.

Ignoring the milk, Bent dug in, slapping a thick steak on his plate and pouring steaming gravy over a slice of hot bread. At the same time, he eyed the Mormon johnnycakes and uncut dried apple pie, wondering how much of the meal he could manage to put himself around this morning.

Nor did Slade have to be prodded.

During the meal, he told Ware of his run-in with the couple by the river.

A frown knitted Ware's brows. "That would be Garth Smith and Sarah Cook."

The announcement meant nothing to Slade who washed down the last of his steak with a big drink of rich, cold milk.

Carrying the large pitcher, Mrs. Ware hurried to his side and refilled his glass. Slade nodded. "Fine vittles, ma'am. I reckon you could spoil a man right fast with this kind of grub."

A rosy blush colored her cheeks. "Joseph has to have solid food. He works mighty hard."

Bent ignored the conversation, too busy spreading a heavy layer of cream on a thick slab of dried apple pie. Slade grinned. "Like I said, ma'am. It's mighty fine. If I was a schoolmaster, I'd put you to the head of the class."

Joseph Ware laughed as Rebecca Ware hurried back to her stove, her cheeks red with blush. The laughter faded from Joseph's face as he turned back to Slade. "Garth Smith has got his cap set for Sarah Cook, but his father is against the marriage because the girl refuses to be sealed."

"Sealed?"

Ware explained. "Those not of our faith can become one of us by becoming a member of our faith, the Latter Day Saints, which is what we call ourselves, Saints. That is what Sarah Cook refuses to do. Until they become a member of our faith, they are not permitted a Mormon Temple sealed marriage."

Slade frowned. "Is such a marriage so important?"

Ware nodded. "To us, yes. You see, we believe there is no hell, only three heavens, one for the heathens, one for non-Mormon Christians, and the third for those Mormons with Mormon Temple sealed marriages. Those of these marriages are future mother and father gods whose earthly unions will endure forever in eternity. And that is a sore spot for Brother Smith in regard to young Sarah. He is one of the counselors in our Stake Presidency."

"This Brother Smith happen to be any kin to Garth?" Slade had a sinking feeling in his stomach that he already knew the answer.

"He is Garth's father."

A wry grin split Slade's weathered face. He glanced at Bent, who looked up from his pie, shrugged, and then returned to the task at hand. "It figures," Slade said. "Seems like a body can't get in the water around here without stirring it up some. This Stake Presidency — that the group that makes the decisions?"

Ware nodded, a faint grin on his face. "Yes."

"And that young feller I put through the

wringer last night is the boy of one of the counselors?"

Ware nodded again, the grin on his face growing broader.

Slade saw Ware's smile. "I don't know what you find so funny, Joseph. Me, I figure this is a good example of closing the barn door after the horse is out."

"Maybe not, Jake. The Stake Presidency is made up of three people, a president and two counselors. Currently, I am the president. Caleb Webb is the other counselor. I can offset Aaron Smith, but I still fear your battle faces great odds, perhaps too great."

"From Caleb Webb?"

"No. Caleb is fair."

"From who, then?"

"From New Gideon itself. The Saints are very suspicious of newcomers."

The regulator clock chimed the half hour. Ware glanced over his shoulder and rose quickly. "Excuse me. It's my day to open the irrigation locks. Finish your breakfast. I'll return later. We'll meet then with the council."

Bent had polished off the last of his pie. Slade rose and said, "We'll walk along with you. After a fine meal like this, I feel the need to walk some of it off." He grinned across the room at Mrs. Ware. Her blush deepened. "Besides," he added, "I'd like to hear more about this young couple. The girl talked like she'd just as soon hightail it out of New Gideon as stay."

Ware nodded. "Her folks died on the trail. She was only a child, so she went to live with Constance Young. I can understand why she would like to leave New Gideon. Our ways are strict, and it is mighty hard on a young woman all alone."

Bent snorted. "Ain't no reason a person need stay if they don't like a place. You wouldn't catch me hanging my hat where I wasn't wanted."

Ware frowned.

Slade said. "No offense intended, Joseph, but your ways are strange to us," said Slade.

Ware laughed again and beckoned them to follow. "Many people have said that very thing, Jake."

Once outside, Bent bit off a twist of tobacco and for several moments relished the taste. Finally, he said, "Don't mean no offense, Joseph, but whereabouts is your other wives? I thought Mormons had heaps of them."

With a crooked grin, Ware explained. "Some do. A select few, those Saints considered more worthy and who desire to have more wives take them." He paused, then

34

added. "I could, but Rebecca is all I wish for."

Shaking his head, Bent switched the chaw to his other cheek. "Yep, I reckon things is a mite different here."

The blacksmith laughed and winked at Slade. "Now, come along. I'll show you our irrigation system. Might not seem like much to you, but we're proud of it. With it, we have managed to keep several thousand acres productive."

Slade followed, but the specter of Counselor Aaron Smith nagged at him.

CHAPTER FOUR

The network of irrigation canals carrying water to the wheat and cornfields impressed Slade, but not as much as the pin-neat village of New Gideon. The town was not a mud and stick hodgepodge of dwellings as most western communities, but framed, lap-straked, and freshly whitewashed. The larger buildings on the interior of the village were of red stone, precisely cut and solidly fitted.

As they returned to the blacksmith's house, Slade saw Sarah Cook crossing the street in their direction. "That's the girl I told you about," he said to Bent and Ware.

Bent hesitated at the front door and nodded to the stable. "You two go on in. I want to check my bay. See about her bruised foot."

Without waiting for a response, Bent left them at the door. Ten minutes later, he returned. Joseph Ware pulled on his jacket, and the three men left for the Council Hall.

Replicated after the broad streets in Salt Lake City, the main streets leading to the interior of the village were wide enough for three four-in-hands, coaches drawn by four horses, to pull side by side.

Slade jerked to a halt as they turned the corner onto the street that led to the Council Hall. "Hold on." His voice was tight with concern.

The three men halted. Down the street, a crowd clustered around the Council Hall, a large, rectangular, single-story building of red stone, with half-a-dozen wood-framed windows looking onto the street.

"What's going on?" Slade dropped his hand to his .44. He flipped the rawhide loop off the hammer.

Ware assessed the situation quickly. "Nothing to worry about," he said. "It's the brethren. They're just curious, that's all. We don't have many visitors."

Slade grunted, but remained wary, figuring such a gathering to be the result of something more than curiosity. Word had probably spread about the lesson in manners he had given the Smith boy.

Crowds spooked him. Seemed like there was always one hothead goading the others into doing something they didn't particularly cotton to. From the corner of his eye, he saw Bent's hand drop to his own revolver.

"Just in case," Bent whispered.

Slade noticed several young boys in the crowd. "Children, too, Joseph?"

With a chuckle, the burly blacksmith replied. "They're members of the priest-hood, Jake. At age twelve, every boy becomes a priest."

Bent scratched his head. "I'll swan. Things sure is different here, Joseph."

"What about the girls? They're not part of all this," Slade asked.

Ware looked around at Slade, a puzzled expression on his craggy face. "No. The state of womanhood is inferior to that of the male, naturally," he replied in an amiable tone that seemed to suggest that such was a simple, universal understanding. "The same as it is everywhere."

Slade and Bent exchanged wry grins. The young half-breed knew several independent young ladies who would take heated exception to such an assumption.

The crowd gave them no trouble. Like the Red Sea, the multitude parted to permit the three men to pass. The interior of the building reminded Slade of a courtroom except, instead of a bench for the judge, there was an unadorned, gate-legged table with three chairs, two already occupied, on the platform.

The remaining two-thirds of the room was filled with wooden benches filled with curious citizens, all male, men and boys, Slade noted. And no women, naturally, he told himself wryly.

Ware stopped by an empty bench in the front of the hall. "Here's where you sit."

Slade nodded.

His words couched in suspicion, Bent asked. "Where you going?"

Grinning, Ware gestured to the front of the room. "Up there. That empty chair. The other two men are counselors. That's Caleb Webb on the left. Aaron Smith is the other counselor. I'm the Stake president. Remember?"

Slade had surmised the latter's identity from the dour expression on Smith's face. He glanced over the sea of faces, pausing momentarily when he saw the battered and bruised features of Garth Smith glaring at him.

With the stoic resignation of the Apache, Slade knew from the look in the young man's eyes that sooner or later, there would be trouble. A hollow-cheeked man next to Garth leaned over and whispered in the young man's ear.

After Ware made the introductions, he summed up the purpose of Slade's visit. A natural salesman, the blacksmith pointed out just how New Gideon would benefit from a relay station.

Assenting murmurs came from the crowd, but Slade ignored them. He kept his eyes on the two men at Joseph Ware's side. Aaron Smith's expression had not changed. In that moment, the young half-breed knew that he would never gain Smith's approval, but the other counselor seemed impressed with Ware's explanation. Maybe he was a fair man. Slade could live with a two-to-one vote.

After Ware completed his explanation, the second counselor spoke. "Mr. Slade, my name is Caleb Webb. What Joseph tells us seems to be quite a windfall for our small community. May I ask why you selected us?"

Remaining seated on the bench, Slade replied. "Like I told Joseph, Mr. Webb. You draw a straight line from Fort Atkinson to El Paso, and you'll slice New Gideon right in two."

Aaron Smith spoke up. "How do we know you speak the truth? Perhaps there is another reason you have come?"

A muttering from the crowd told Slade that there had indeed been much speculation as to the real purpose of his visit, much of it probably fired by the beating he had given Garth Smith.

A wry grin curled Slade's lips. "Maybe you can tell me, Mr. Smith. What reason could I have?"

"Lucifer, the evil brother of Jesus, is the father of lies and of wickedness. He is always among us in various disguises, Mr. Slade."

Ware shot Slade a concerned look. Slade's grin widened. "I reckon old Scratch would have to be mighty hard up to come out looking like me, Mr. Smith."

The crowd laughed. Aaron Smith's craggy face darkened. "We do not treat the Devil with levity, Mr. Slade. We gird up our loins to battle daily with him and struggle against the many temptations he and his horde of followers place in our path. You and those like you are the spawn of Lucifer."

Slade's cheeks burned. He clenched his fists.

Bent leaned over and whispered into the younger man's ear. "What in the hell is that idiot talking about?"

A voice from the rear of the room shouted. "How do we know he ain't one of them rustlers come in here to size up our stock? Maybe catch us off guard."

A few mutters of assent rose from the crowd.

Slade looked around. The speaker was the hollow-cheeked man next to Garth Smith. The man glanced around the room, seeking support. "I figure them two rode in here just to see what kind of strength we got. How do we know he ain't got an army of renegades hidin' out on the prairie just awaiting his signal to ride in and massacre ever' last one of us?"

Bent jumped up, but Slade's hand on the old man's arm stayed him. The young half-breed eyed the speaker with contempt. His voice chilled the room when he replied. "Mister, I don't know who you are, but if you believe that, you got more dumb in you than a dog has fleas. The only reason I don't put knots on your head is because Joseph Ware has treated me fine. You can thank him for that."

Bent, still standing, nodded his agreement.

The skinny man stuck out his jaw. "I don't have to thank Joseph Ware or no man for nothing. And I certain ain't afraid of no man who sneaks up on a man and his woman and coldcocks him with his pistol."

Slade shot Garth Smith a glance. The younger man dropped his eyes. The skinny man continued, speaking to the crowd. "Look at him. He's part Injun, which means he's gotta be one of them rustlers. A coward and a thief — that's what he is, nothing but a low-down, conniving —"

Bent stepped forward and slammed a large fist into the skinny man's jaw. The man's head whipped to the right with such force that his body spun to the floor.

Slade jumped in front of Bent and pushed the older man away. Instantly, hands grabbed for Slade. He felt his vest tear as he was yanked around. Fists pummeled him. Whirling, he struck out at the first face he saw, grunting with satisfaction as his bony fist caught his attacker square between the eyes. He didn't want a fight, but he sure wasn't about to back away from one.

A fist glanced off Slade's shoulder. He spun to the right, swinging his cocked elbow behind him as he did. The point of his elbow struck bone, which cracked. Stunned grunts and cries sounded in his ears. He hammered furiously at the onslaught of men even as he absorbed their blows. Warm blood trickled down his chin.

A blow from the back caught Slade on the side of his head and staggered him. His knees buckled, but he shook off the blow and turned on his attacker, throwing a wicked left hook.

The smug grin on Garth Smith's face froze when he saw that his sneaky punch had failed to stop Slade. From the corner of his eye, he saw Slade's blow coming, but his feet refused to move. In the next instant, stars exploded in his head, and a wave of blackness swept over him.

Aaron Smith's voice cut through the melee of battle. "Garth!"

The booming explosion of a .44 halted the battle in midstride. Three-Fingers Bent had backed into one corner of the room and, smoking revolver in hand, stood glaring at the crowd. "That's it, boys. Just back away," he said in his soft, laconic voice.

Slade scooped up his hat and pulled his own gun. Anger flashed in his eyes as he backed away from the suddenly silent crowd of men. He threw a crooked grin at Bent. "About time. Things was getting mighty busy out here."

Using the muzzle of his revolver, Bent motioned the men away from the door. "Clear a path out there, boys." Reluctantly, the men moved away from the door, their glowering faces tight with anger.

"Hold it," cautioned Slade.

Bent frowned. "For what?"

He nodded to the crowd outside the door.

"Them," Slade said. "We'd never make it out of here." He glanced across the room at Joseph Ware whose face reflected embarrassment and chagrin at the way his guests had been treated. Standing beside Ware, Aaron Smith glared at them like an Old Testament prophet ready to cast the unrepentant sinner into hell.

"What do you reckon on doing?" asked Bent.

Slade's brain raced. Forget the relay station, he told himself. Their first job was to get the hell away from New Gideon and all these damned Saints as they called themselves. "I figure on fogging out of here as fast as our ponies will take us."

Bent grunted. "You ain't gettin' no argument from me, but just how do you figure to go about it? I got the feeling they ain't going to let us just lollygag our way out of here."

The young half-breed eyed the crowd of men across the room. They glared back, fists doubled, jaws set, like a pack of wolves waiting for just the right moment. Slade moved to the front of the room, his deerskin moccasins making no sound on the puncheon floor.

He paused in front of Joseph Ware. "I didn't plan for this to happen, Joseph."

Ware shook his head slowly. His large shoulders slumped. "I didn't either, Jake. I'm sorry."

Without replying, Slade turned to the two men by Ware's side, Caleb Webb and Aaron Smith. He jammed the muzzle of his .44 under Aaron Smith's chin. "Like it or not, you two are taking us to the stable."

Caleb Webb's face blanched with fear even as Aaron Smith's face darkened in anger. "God will punish you for this. This is a sin against —"

Slade cut him off. "I got no time for sermons now. And I reckon He'll whup up on me just like I'll whup up on you two if you don't shut up and start walking."

"Jake!" Joseph Ware's face was unbelieving.

"I don't plan on doing hurt to anyone, Joseph. But I plan on getting out of this little piece of hell you call a town or die trying. And if I go down," he added, "They'll be a bunch goes with me."

An undercurrent of mutters filled the room.

"Bent, you poke your hogleg in the middle of Webb's back and follow me out." Slade waved the muzzle of the .44. "Now, let's go."

Bent fell behind Caleb Webb. "Move," he

growled. His eyes darting from side to side, he muttered, "I got me a spanking new twenty-dollar gold piece says we don't make it." He spoke the words to Slade, but they were loud enough for every man in the room to hear and to remember.

"I'll take that bet," Slade said over his shoulder, his face frozen in granite.

Outside, the crowd drew back. Dark murmurs spread throughout the throng, which followed the four men at a respectful distance. Once or twice, Aaron Smith stumbled. The muttering of the crowd swelled, then lapsed back into silence as he quickly regained his feet.

Five minutes later, Slade, with Bent at his side, dug his heels into the blue roan's flanks and raced out of New Gideon. Bending low over their galloping animals, the two men did not slacken their speed until they reached the rim of the valley.

Nana was waiting for them. Pausing to breathe their horses, Slade quickly related the events of the last several hours while keeping watch on their back trail.

Bent tore off a chuck of tobacco. "So now what?"

Slade shrugged. "We still need to spot a suitable place for a relay station around here somewhere."

Nana, a leather-tough Apache a head shorter than Slade disagreed. "No, Busca. I have a bad feeling of this place. We —" He gestured to the three of them. "We will be safe away from here — back among the peaks of the great mountains — back in Arizona." He nodded to Slade. "That is where the One-Who-Seeks belongs. Not here," he added, gesturing with disdain to the valley below.

For several moments, Slade considered his Apache brother's words. His own mother had been a Nez Perce princess. After her murder and the kidnapping of his sister, Mimbre Apaches found him and nursed him back to health. He lived with them until he was fifteen and had the same respect for their beliefs as they.

So Nana's concern worried him, but he had promised Bill Harnden that he would find locations for their relay stations. He glanced over his shoulder down into the valley. And his own life savings was at stake also.

New Gideon was a speck in the distance. The sky was blue, and the air was still. Their own dust had settled, and there was none below to indicate any pursuit.

"I say we listen to Nana," Bent said. "These Mormon folk are right unpredictable, and mighty unfriendly."

Slade studied his two friends as he pondered his decision. He had too much at stake to give up now. All they needed was one more location. Finally, he said, "First, let's follow the river back north. Find a place for a relay station before heading back to El Paso. From there, we head for Arizona Territory."

Nana said nothing, but the frown on his face spoke volumes.

Bent grunted. "Well then, I figure we oughta just eyeball these places at a gallop."

A grin spread over Slade's face. "Don't worry, old man. Poking along isn't my strong suit."

The three men spent that evening and the next morning inspecting a few shallow crossings in the Canadian River to determine which one would prove the most satisfactory site for a swing station. By noon, they had found three sites, each with its own drawbacks as well as advantages.

Abruptly, Nana drew up his mustang, a close-coupled animal with long hair. "Someone comes," he said simply.

At Nana's words, Slade nodded and led the way into a thicket of cedar on a bluff overlooking the river and dismounted. Minutes later, a string of riders appeared. Slade did not recognize the first rider, but he saw plainly that Joseph Ware was the second. Behind the blacksmith came more men, some of whom Slade recognized, not by name, but because they had been part of the fight the day before. Bringing up the rear was Aaron Smith and his son, Garth.

The riders dismounted in a cottonwood grove and started a small fire for the noon meal.

Glancing over his shoulder, Slade saw that Nana had disappeared. Moments later, he glimpsed the lithe figure of his Apache brother slipping through the underbrush near the grove.

Thirty minutes later, the men rode on. Moments later, Nana returned.

Looping the rawhide thong back over the hammer of his .44, Slade asked, "What's it all about?"

"It's Bent," the Apache said. "They want Bent."

Slade frowned at the older man. "For what?"

"Murder. They come after Bent for killing a man."

CHAPTER FIVE

Bent sagged like he had been struck between the eyes with a singletree. He tried to speak, but the words stuck in his throat.

Slade and Nana looked at each other. An unspoken understanding passed between them. That Bent was guilty was not even considered. Someone was swinging a wide loop with Bent's name on it, and both Slade and Nana knew the smartest move for the three was to hightail it back to El Paso, pick up Bill Harnden, and then head out for the territory. Any of the three sites they had inspected for a relay station would serve its purpose despite the proximity to New Gideon. When Slade later returned to build the station, Bent would remain behind in Tucson.

The Apache grabbed his mustang's mane and swung astride the small gray pony. Slade did the same. "Come on, Bent. Let's us light a shuck out of here."

The grizzled old man shifted his chaw of tobacco to his other cheek. "Wait a damned minute there."

Slade wheeled the blue roan around. "For what? Those jaspers are going to swing south sooner or later. Come night, we best be long gone out of here."

"But I didn't kill nobody." He punctuated his denial with an arc of tobacco.

Nana listened impassively to the exchange. "Hell, I know you didn't."

"Then I ain't runnin'."

The young half-breed studied the older man with the same stolid expression with which Nana regarded the two of them. "Why not?" He had a sinking feeling in the pit of his stomach. He had batched with Bent for the last several years, and he knew just how stubborn the old man could be — like a winter-gaunted grizzly.

" 'Cause I didn't do it."

Slade tried to argue. "I know that, but these folks aren't the kind you reason with. You saw that back at the Council Hall." He hesitated. Bent said nothing. Slade continued. "Look at them, Bent. What with them claiming people turn into gods. And that there's no hell." He shook his head. "I tell you, Bent, a steer with a bellyful of loco weed's got more sense than them folks."

Bent nodded. "They is crazy for a fact."

Encouraged, Slade continued. "All I'm saying is that let's get back to Arizona Territory where we belong. They'll find the real killer sooner or later."

For a moment, Slade thought he had convinced Bent, but the older man snorted. "I don't cotton to the idea of always wondering when some marshal is gonna come in with a warrant for somethin' I didn't do. You damned well know what that feeling is like. Remember Jack Barker?"

A sense of frustration washed over Slade. "Dammit, Bent, you know as well as boils on old Bill's butt that the law can't come into Arizona Territory after anybody. Old Jack never came after me. At least, not more than once. And then he was breaking the law."

Bent shook his head and loosed a stream of tobacco for emphasis. "I ain't goin' to wait."

The muscles in his jaw twisting like a den of snakes, Slade glared at the mulish old man. "I swear, Bent, if you're not the hard-headedest old coot I —"

Before Slade could finish, Bent pulled out his .44 and fired off three fast shots into the air.

"Bent! You damned idiot." Slade shot

Nana a look.

The Apache nodded and wheeled his pony about, quickly disappearing into the underbrush.

Bent holstered his revolver and stared levelly at his younger friend. "I ain't never run from nothing, and I sure as hell don't plan on doing it now." With those words, he turned his bay toward the river.

In the distance came the sound of pounding hoofs.

With a slow shake of his head, Slade followed Bent down to the river. The Indian in Slade understood Bent's decision. The white man in Slade cursed Bent's foolishness.

The two men sat astride their horses watching as the riders rounded the bend in the river and spied them. With a wild shout, the Mormons spurred their horses toward the waiting men.

Slade kept his eyes on the approaching riders, but he said to Bent. "Let me do the talking, you hear?"

"I can handle it."

"Don't argue. Don't say nothing."

Bent grunted. "But —"

"I'll explain later."

When the Mormons were less than fifty yards away, Slade fired into the air, then lowered his .44 Colt to cover the oncoming riders. The horses slid to a halt. The riders glanced at each other, puzzled as to their next step. They had the man they were after. Or did he have them?

Aaron Smith pushed to the front, his craggy face flushed with success. "You can put up your revolver, Mr. Slade. It is not you we seek. We've come for Mr. Bent." He started forward, but halted when Slade cocked the hammer.

"Hold it, Smith. Nobody's taking Bent anywhere."

Joseph Ware rode up beside Aaron Smith. "There's trouble, Jake. We got questions that need answers."

His face like granite, Slade asked, "What kind of questions?"

Ware drew a deep breath. "There's been some big trouble in New Gideon."

Bent broke in. "The onliest questions I'll answer for the lot of you is that I didn't kill nobody."

Jake cringed inwardly at Bent's words.

Aaron Smith grinned, a thin, gloating twist of his lips. "We said nothing of a killing."

Suddenly aware of what Slade had tried to tell him, the old man glanced at his young friend in alarm.

The crowd of riders eased forward, an undercurrent of satisfied murmurs evidence that they had indeed apprehended the killer.

Slade's voice cut through the muttering. "I said, hold it. Rein those ponies up if you don't want hot lead."

Joseph Ware spoke. "Easy, Jake. Tell me, then. How did Bent know about the murder? It happened last night, before midnight. Somebody stabbed Wiley Bledsoe to death. Drove the blade clean through him."

Slade fixed his eyes on the blacksmith. "Bent was with me last night. We camped back down on the Canadian."

"That ain't what Joseph asked. Besides, he could have slipped away while you slept," Aaron Smith growled.

The young half-breed studied the hard-faced group of men. They were determined to take somebody back to New Gideon, and Bent's denial had tossed the old man right into their hands.

He looked at Joseph Ware but spoke loudly enough for the others to hear. "I lived with the Apache for almost eight years when I was just a button. My Apache brother is with me. When you camped for noon, he slipped in and heard you all palavering."

Aaron Smith snorted. "Likely story."

"Yeah," echoed another voice, growing

more confident. "Let's take them both back to the judge."

But no one moved as a profound silence filled the air.

Slade cupped his hand and gave the call of a whippoorwill. At the end of the call, he added the coo of a dove.

No sooner had the echoes of the cry died away than Nana, like a ghost, appeared from the underbrush astride his mustang. His Winchester rested in the crook of his arm.

Excited murmurs came from the riders.

Slade said to Ware, "I don't lie, Joseph. Bent didn't kill anyone. He was with us last night. Besides, the only knife he owns is a barlow, and it won't go more than a couple inches into a jasper."

Ware sighed and said, "I want to believe you, but there's a piece of evidence that can't be explained away." He fastened his eyes on Three-Fingers Bent coldly. "Something that points directly to Mr. Bent."

"Like what?" demanded Bent.

Aaron Smith fished in the pocket of his broadcloth coat and held a coin over his head. The rays of the overhead sun bounced off the coin with a brilliant luster. "This. Found on the floor in Wiley Bledsoe's house. A twenty-dollar gold piece."

A frown knit Slade's brows. "Just who is

this Wiley Bledsoe yahoo?" He asked of Joseph Ware.

The big blacksmith met Slade's eyes. "He's the one who denounced you yesterday." He cut his eyes toward Bent. "He's the one Bent struck in the Council Hall."

"And no one in all of New Gideon owns a gold coin, especially a twenty-dollar gold piece," chimed in Aaron Smith.

Bent said. "Well, I didn't kill him. Besides, how do you figure that gold piece is mine?"

Garth Smith yelled back. "You was the one talking about a gold piece back at the Council Hall."

Several voices echoed agreement.

Slade interrupted. "Just because some hombre mentions a gold piece proves nothing. The killer could have been one of your own people. You've got no idea what some people might have stuck back in a fruit jar or rat-holed in a pot. Everybody's got gold coins."

Garth Smith pushed his sorrel through the cluster of riders until he reached his father's side. "Don't listen to him, Pa. We got the one who did it. Let's take him back to the judge."

The riders muttered their agreement. One shouted above the confusion of voices. "I say, let's take care of him right now. He's the one what killed Wiley." The man waved a lariat over his head.

Before anyone could reply, the crack of a rifle split the air. The man screamed as the slug ripped the lariat from his hand. Instantly, the riders grew silent, their eyes fastened on the impassive Apache sitting astride his mustang. Slowly, Nana lowered his Winchester.

Slade used the distraction to back his horse away. Bent did likewise. They halted several yards away. When Slade spoke, the men jumped. "That's why we're not going back. You righteous people already got your mind made up." He shook his head, his gray eyes blazing anger like a pitch fire. "Whoever killed Wiley Bledsoe is in New Gideon, unless," he added, letting his eyes play over each man. "Unless, he's riding with you right now."

The men glanced around at each other, clearing their throats uncomfortably.

The young half-breed spoke to Bent, but he kept his eyes on Aaron Smith. "You see what I meant about these people, Bent? You can't go back there. They'll railroad you to the nearest tree."

Joseph Ware spoke up. "There'll be no railroading as long as I'm there." He turned in his saddle and looked at the men behind him. "Any man who tries will answer to me."

Before anyone could reply, Bent spoke up. "I'm going back."

His words stunned Slade. "You're what?"

Bent worked the tobacco in his mouth into a ball and spit it out on the sand at his pony's feet. "Look, boy. I never done nothing wrong in my life — well, at least, nothing bad wrong that woulda put me in jail for any length of time. I didn't do this either. I ain't particularly religious, but I noticed all my life that if a feller does right, he generally ends up okay."

Aaron Smith grinned in smug satisfaction. "Now you're talking sense." He rode forward, his hand outstretched. "Let me have your gun. You're under arrest for the murder of Wiley Bledsoe."

Chapter Six

The boom of the .44 racketed in their ears, and a chunk of sand exploded in front of Aaron Smith's horse. The animal squealed and reared up on his hind legs, pawing at the fleecy clouds overhead. Smith tumbled backward out of the saddle, landing on the sand.

Slade cocked his six-shooter. "No one takes my gun or Bent's." His cold voice cut through the turmoil. "Bent goes back on his own choice, not because he's arrested. First man who tries anything, and I mean anything, will find a mighty ugly hole between his eyes when he looks in the mirror. And don't try nothing behind our backs. You do . . ." His voice died away as he nodded to Nana who disappeared back into the underbrush.

Aaron Smith scrambled to his feet and grabbed the reins of his spooked animal. "How do we know we can trust you to do what you say?"

Slade's words were cold and hostile. "I'm not the one to worry about trusting, Aaron Smith. You're the one that folks best keep an eye on." His eyes, like ice, narrowed with promise. "You just remember this. Anything happens to Bent, I'll come after you first, and then your boy and then all of your wives."

For several seconds, a deathly silence filled the air.

During the ride back to New Gideon, Slade argued with Bent. "You're crazy to go back."

Scratching his graying beard, the old mountain man shrugged. "Don't have a lot of choice." Slade frowned, and Bent continued. "That Sarah Cook girl — you remember her?"

"Yeah."

He lowered his voice. "Well, I gave her a twenty-dollar gold piece yesterday morning when we came back from irrigating. You said she wanted to get away from there, so I figured I'd help her."

With a wry grin, Slade muttered. "So that's it. You figure that she might be blamed."

"What do you think?" His question was couched with gentle sarcasm. "Considering just how crazy these here people be."

The wiry young half-breed eyed the riders ahead of them. "I figure you could be right."

They rode in silence. After a few miles, Slade mumbled to Bent. "You got any more of those gold pieces?"

"That was my last one. Why?"

Garth Smith rode up beside them, cutting off their conversation. Slade, like Bent, did not even consider the possibility of Sarah Cook committing the murder. When Bent revealed his actions, Slade's initial impulse was to tell the posse, but something made him hesitate.

He decided that it would be better to wait until they reached New Gideon. All they had to do then was have Sarah Cook confirm Bent's words, and perhaps display the coin. That should take care of all questions.

They rode into New Gideon just before dusk. Slade spied Sarah Cook strolling along the riverbank. His thoughts were interrupted when Joseph Ware offered them a room at his place. Slade refused, bitter toward the prejudice of the Mormons. Bent grinned. "Then you sleep in the stable. Me, I'm staying inside on a real bed."

After a hot meal, Slade excused himself to check on the horses, after which he sauntered casually in front of Constance Young's house, hoping that he might run into Sarah Cook. The streets were empty. Finally, he decided to wait until the following day, fearing that a night call would raise other questions, questions that could lead to incriminating answers.

Inside the blacksmith's neat house, Ware and Bent sat in front of the small fire. "I don't like the idea of Jake being outside after dark," said the blacksmith, genuine concern in his voice. "These people are good people, but there are a couple hotheads around like Garth Smith, and some of the Saints are easily led."

Bent cackled. "You don't got to worry none about Jake. I've knowed him seven-eight years now. He can more than take up for hisself. Why, he's got more Indian in him than even a full-blood."

"That why he spends so much time by himself? I noticed that he slept outside that first night here."

Bent scooted back and forth in the easy chair, settling deep into its softness. "Some, but he's one of them that thinks, and worries. You see, when he was about seven or eight and his old man was dead, Comancheros raided his home, killed his mama, and kidnapped his baby sister. Shot him and left him for dead, but a Mimbre Apache found him and took him back to the rancheria where they nursed him back to health. He grew up with the Apache. Why, one of the braves who learnt Jake about Injun ways was Gokhlayeh, the one they call Geronimo."

Ware's wife had taken a nearby chair and listened as Bent continued. "Jake's mama was a Nez Perce princess. In fact, what I learned among the Injuns was that the Nez Perce was sorta like what you call ariso— ariecat—"

Mrs. Ware supplied the word Bent was searching for. "Aristocrats?"

He grinned and nodded to her. "That's it. Much obliged, ma'am. Well, the Nez Perce was the aristocrats among the Injuns. Anyways, Jake, he grew up with the Apache, learned all their ways and customs and beliefs."

"That's why that Indian follows him around?" Ware gestured outside with the stem of his pipe.

"They're brothers. I reckon they sort of follow each other around."

Ware nodded, and Bent went on to tell of how Slade had served in the War of Secession with J. E. B. Stuart and Joe Wheeler and Bedford Forrest, and then of the numerous journeys and travails around the southwest and into Mexico in search of his kidnapped sister until this past winter when they were finally reunited. He even told them about the shootout down in Brazoria country and Lawman Jack Barker's dogged pursuit of the young man until witnesses testified to Slade's innocence.

"He's mighty young to have experienced all that he has," noted Ware thoughtfully when Bent finished.

"In years, I reckon you're right. I don't know if you folks know what it's like out here or not, but if you ain't a man at twelve or thirteen, chances are you ain't never goin' to make it."

The next morning, Slade and Bent accompanied Ware to the Council Hall. Scanning the valley, Slade nudged Bent. The older man grinned when he saw the dark object moving slowly along the rim. Nana.

Earlier, during breakfast, Slade had questioned Ware about the rustlers, about Wiley Bledsoe, about Garth Smith, about several others, Sarah Cook included, although his questions concerning her were deliberately cursory. Sooner or later, he could get her alone. Then he could ask his questions.

After breakfast when he and Bent were

alone, Slade told the older man of his plan. "Once she shows the town the coin you gave her, they'll have to turn you loose. Until then, don't say anything about her."

Bent grinned. "I hope you're right." He tugged his hat on his head as they left the house. Outside, Joseph Ware waited.

Before they entered the Council Hall, Slade revealed his belief to Ware that the murder was somehow connected with the rustling.

"What makes you think that, Jake?"

"I been giving it a lot of thought, and I don't know what else it could be. I know the idea's mighty thin, but for a fact, Bent didn't kill Bledsoe. The only other trouble you've had around here has been with the rustlers."

Ware frowned. "They hit us last time about a month before you and Bent showed up. Luckily, they missed a couple hundred head we had grazing in a small valley up river."

Slade tucked Ware's last remark back into the fast growing repository of miscellaneous facts. He said. "Now, I want you folks to remember that Bent came back on his own. So what I want from you and yours, Joseph, is time to dig through all this and find the truth. That might call for me to be gone a

67

good spell. If I am, I want your word that Bent stays with you, under your protection, and," he added firmly, "he keeps his six-gun."

Ware nodded vigorously. "Certainly. But do you have anything to go on?"

Ruefully, Slade shook his head as he climbed the steps into the Council Hall. "Only that I know Bent."

The meeting went as Slade had hoped. Despite some muttering and misgivings, the Stake Council granted the young man's request, but only after Joseph Ware was forced to place his reputation and authority as Stake President up as a trade-off should Slade and Bent skip out.

After the meeting, Slade sent Bent back to the blacksmith's house despite the older man's complaining. "I've got a lot of snooping around to do, Bent. Folks might get nervous should they see you out wandering around. Me, they'll notice, but they won't pay me much mind after a few days."

Ware agreed with Slade's assessment.

With Bent safely settled in at the blacksmith's enjoying a midmorning snack of freshly baked sweet potato pie and fresh cream, Slade and Ware paid a visit to Wiley Bledsoe's house, a small, two-room frame, much like every other house in the community.

Joseph Ware jerked to a halt when he opened the door and shook his head. "Would you look at this?"

The cabin was not the rough and Spartan quarters as suited most Mormon bachelors. The front room was living area and kitchen while the rear room contained a hand-hewn cottonwood bed, which took up almost the entire room. Along one wall in the bedroom, an odd assortment of store-bought work clothes, two broadcloth suits, and a new Stetson hung on clothes hooks. Two pairs of new work boots sat on the simple puncheon floor.

Back in the front room, Slade looked around. "Anyone been in here?"

Ware shook his head, still amazed at the furnishings. "Only to take care of the body. My wife straightened the house a little."

"So nobody took anything out?"

"Nope, though to be honest, after Rebecca had cleaned the place up, she told me that she powerfully admired some of his furnishings, especially the coal oil lamp."

Slade paused by the table in the middle of the room and picked up the lamp, the chimney of which was etched with flowers, and the blue base of which was cut glass. It was fancy, fancier than any lamp Slade had ever seen.

Replacing the lamp, Slade noticed a small pile of odds and ends on the table. "Wonder where he got the lamp?" he muttered as he rummaged through the small pile.

"Wiley traveled around a good bit after he came here five-six years back. Probably just picked it up somewhere. Not much of a farmer. He was a good man in his way, but there were some of us did wonder at times about his dedication and consecration."

Growing suspicious, Slade remarked, "Look at this." He held a cased gold watch. He flipped the cover open to reveal a watch face with filigreed gold numbers. He glanced at Ware. "I don't figure he *just* picked this up."

Against the wall sat a small chest of drawers with a round mirror above. On the bench next to the chest was a tilting water pitcher of blue and white porcelain that reminded Slade of a human torso with armless shoulders resting on fulcrums and a handle to tilt the basin and pour from the neck. "I saw a few fancy hotels during the war, but I never saw a water pitcher like this."

"Me neither," the blacksmith said over Slade's shoulder.

Slade started to turn back to Joseph Ware when he noticed the floor at the base of the chest. A thin crack ran at a right angle to the seams between the planks in the floor and disappeared under the chest. Slade knelt. "Is Mrs. Ware one of those that moves furniture around when she cleans?" He ran his finger along the crack.

Ware laughed. "More'n any woman I ever known. Rebecca, she gets mighty fidgety when there's even a speck of dust on the floor."

Without replying, Slade scooted the chest aside, revealing a trapdoor about a foot square in the floor. He sat back on his heels and slipped his knife from its sheath. "Wonder what we have here."

"What do you mean?" Ware looked over his shoulder. "What is it?"

"Don't rightly know, but if I was to take a guess, I'd say Wiley Bledsoe had him his own private safe." He dug the point of the knife into the crack and popped the door open. The musty smell of earth rolled up, and beneath the floor was a small tin bucket.

Slade picked it up by the wire handle and looked at Joseph Ware, who muttered in surprise. "A lard bucket?"

Slade read the label. "A. W. Jacobs. Warranted Pure Lard. Greeley, Colorado."

Ware looked at Slade. "What do you make of it?"

"It appears Mr. Bledsoe had a few other belongings, some that he didn't want anyone to know about," he said as he set the bucket on the table and popped open the lid.

A soft whistle escaped Ware's lips when he saw the contents of the bucket. Rolls of paper currency, Union bills, filled the bucket to the brim.

CHAPTER SEVEN

For several seconds, neither man spoke. Glancing over his shoulder, Slade replaced the lid and returned the bucket to its repository under the floor. He slid the chest back over the entire trapdoor and looked around at Ware, who had plopped down in one of the straight back chairs, his eyes fixed on the floor beneath the chest.

Stepping quickly to a window, Slade scanned the area around the house. "I figure we'd best be going. We stay too long, someone might get suspicious that we found something."

Ware frowned, then nodded his understanding. With a last glance at the chest of drawers, he followed Slade outside where the young half-breed knelt and studied the ground below the bedroom window. There were brogan tracks. The edges were indistinct. He pointed at them. "Look at that one."

Ware studied it. The print indicated that the heel of the right brogan had picked up a bent horseshoe nail. "I see it."

Slade frowned. Something was bothering him, something that he had overlooked, but what? The idea evaded him, playing just beyond the periphery of his grasp. "I reckon it's time to get back to the house. We got some talking to do. There's questions that need some answering."

Joseph Ware fumbled for words as he stared across the supper table at Slade, who was spooning gravy over the wedge of home-made bread and a thick slab of fried steak on his plate. "You — you can't be serious. Wiley Bledsoe might have had his failings like all of us, but I can't believe that he was in with the rustlers. That's — that's —" He shrugged his massive shoulders in disbelief.

"Then tell me where he came by that money," Slade replied, sensitive to the older man's distraught feelings. "Think about it, Joseph. Here's a man who claimed to be just a farmer, and not a very good one, you said. You saw for yourself that he had possessions that most of us would just dream of having. How did he pay for them all?"

Frowning, Joseph Ware shook his head. "I don't know, but there must be some explanation, some reason in all this madness. He was one of the brethren, a Saint."

"Excuse me for saying so, Joseph, but the brethren be damned. He was a man," said Slade. "You said it earlier, we all got our failings."

Bent cleared his throat and joined the discussion. "You really reckon he was one of the rustlers?"

A wry grin spread over Slade's face. "I wouldn't guarantee anything. But, right now, I figure that's one of our options." He speared a square of steak and shook the fork to emphasize his theory. "Here's how I see it, Joseph. You folks been hit several times in the last half-dozen years."

"That's right."

"And you said earlier that Bledsoe had come here five or six years ago."

Ware nodded.

Slade asked. "How long after that did the rustling start?"

The burly blacksmith frowned. "I hadn't thought of that. A couple months, I reckon."

"How many head of beef you lost?"

"Last time was about fifty. I reckon they stole three or four hundred over the years."

Slade suppressed a grin. A few pieces were falling in place. "There's no way Bledsoe could have rat-holed a lard can full of money from just your beef. That means he had to be in on more than just helping the rustlers take your cattle. I'd give you odds that each time he went on one of those *trips* of his, someone, somewhere, lost some stock. There's a passel of herds pushing up to Dodge and beyond."

Bent nodded.

Ware shook his head. "Seems like you're stretching your supposes mighty thin."

Slade shrugged. "Sometimes, you got to."

"Suppose you are right. How can you prove any of them, at least, good enough to convince the judge?"

"I can't," the leather-tough young man replied. "Not yet. But give me time." He sounded confident, but his confidence was riddled with dozens of questions, most unanswered and some not yet formed.

That night, Slade met Nana several miles up river. Quickly, he related all that had taken place in New Gideon as well as his own suspicions. Next, he outlined his plan, flawed as it was.

Nana grunted. "We will find them, Busca."

Slade laid his hand on his brother's shoulder. "It's the only chance Bent has. We'll head north. Their sign will be old. Maybe hard to cut."

A broad grin split Nana's pan-shaped face, revealing glistening white teeth. "You have forgotten when we were boys. We could track even the rabbit."

"*You* could track the rabbit. Not me."

"Busca does me honor, but it was not to I that the great Mangas Coloradas gave much praise."

The two men stared warmly at each other. Slade's face grew serious. "I'll ride with you until we cut their sign. Then you trail them. That will give me time to follow up on one or two loose ends back in New Gideon," replied Slade, remembering Sarah Cook's evening strolls along the riverbank. He wanted to talk to her in private. No sense in causing her any unnecessary trouble. From what he surmised from the first night he ran into her and Garth Smith, she had about all the trouble she could handle.

He figured that the people in the small village, while basically good, God-fearing folks, were probably like most people in other small villages, slaves to petty gossip and rumors. If they heard that she was even questioned, they would never forget, nor would they let her forget.

They cut the rustler's sign at mid-afternoon, then parted after planning to meet within the next couple days.

■ ■ ■ ■

Slade reached New Gideon just before dusk. He pulled up at the river's edge and removed a shirt from his saddlebags. He knelt on the shore under the pretense of washing the light-colored linen shirt, hoping Sarah Cook would stroll by.

He was in luck.

Within minutes after he squatted by the riverbank, he heard the crunch of gravel beneath feet. Slade glanced up, his eyes meeting Sarah Cook's as she jerked to a surprised halt. Her hand flew to her mouth.

Slade rose quickly, a faint smile on his lips. "Didn't mean to frighten you, Miss Cook." He hastened to add, "And I certainly didn't mean to scare you the other night. I just don't cotton to men pushing women around."

The fear faded from her face as she recognized him. "Thank you, Mr. Slade. That was very gallant of you."

It was Slade's turn to be surprised. "You know my name."

A becoming smile brightened her scrubbed-clean face. "Everyone in New Gideon knows of you and Mr. Bent." She arched an eyebrow at the shirt in his hands.

He held up the wet shirt. "Just trying to remove a little dirt," he said, grinning to put her at ease.

She studied the shirt with knowing eyes. "Without soap?" Her reply exuded confidence. She was sure of herself, like a mother with an unruly and stubborn child.

The girl was a sharp one. For several seconds, they stared into each other's eyes, one recognizing that his ploy had been discovered, and the other curious as to why he had even attempted it in the first place.

"Suppose I told you that I always used rocks to clean my clothes when I was on the move? The Indian way." There was a challenge in his tone.

Her eyes assessed the clothes he was wearing. "I'd say then that you wasted a lot of money." A teasing smile played over her lips, and her eyes danced. Before Slade could reply, Sarah Cook added. "For a plainsman, Mr. Slade, you don't use your eyes like you should." She nodded to his shirt, a loosely knit linen. "Even in the bad light, I can see it's not threadbare, which it would be if you used the rocks to clean it."

He glanced down at his shirt, then back at her. "I might say I bought it before leaving Tucson."

She pursed her lips and arched her eyebrows. "You might. Did you?"

With a broad grin, he shook his head. "Well, lady, I reckon you've seen clear through my poor attempt to hide my reason for being here. And to be honest, I'm mighty relieved myself. Sneaking around don't come too easy for me."

Sarah returned his smile. "Then suppose you tell me why you concocted this charade just to meet with me, Mr. Slade."

He squeezed the water from the dripping shirt and rolled it into a ball. "I reckon you know someone done in Wiley Bledsoe. And you probably know by now that my friend, Bent, is the one they figure did it."

Sarah nodded, her eyes narrowing. There was a nervous edge to her voice. "So I've heard. What does it have to do with me?"

Slade studied her. His earlier subterfuge had not fooled her. She was a bright woman, too bright not to figure that he wanted to talk to her about the twenty-dollar gold piece. No sense in mincing words, he decided. "He gave you a gold coin that morning before we went to the Council Hall, remember?"

"I remember," she replied, clipping her words. She set her jaw against her wavering confidence.

"And you know they found a twenty-dollar gold piece by Wiley Bledsoe?"

Her shoulders slumped, her face crumbled as she lost her composure. "I know. I hoped they wouldn't catch Mr. Bent — that he would escape. But if they did, I hoped nobody would say anything about the coin."

"Why not?"

She cleared her throat. "Well, it would cause a problem."

A rueful grin curled his lips at her understatement. "I reckon it's done just that, Miss Cook."

"Not the kind of problem you're thinking about."

A frown knit his eyebrows. "I don't follow you."

She dropped her gaze. "You see, I don't have the coin."

Her announcement caught him unexpectedly. "Don't have it?"

The young girl looked up at him, her eyes asking him to believe her. "No. I took it home where I live with Constance Young. I thought I placed it in my keepsake tin on the nightstand. When I heard about Mr. Bledsoe, I looked, but the coin had vanished." She shook her head. "I would have sworn I put it in the tin box, but I must have been mistaken."

"So you kept quiet?"

The red glow from the setting sun reflected off the tears forming in her eyes. "I know it was wrong, but I was scared. I didn't know what else to do, and I didn't have anybody to go to for advice."

Slade bit off the sharp reply forming in his throat. He studied Sarah Cook's distraught face. He could understand why she would be scared. A young sixteen-, maybe seventeen-year-old woman with no family, no one to turn to for help or support.

Hell, he'd had a whole tribe of family to look after him from the great Mangas Coloradas down to his Apache brothers, Nana and Paleto. He'd had family to turn to, but she . . . His thoughts became confused, and a chilling thought leaped into his head. Was it possible she killed Bledsoe?

He studied her a moment longer. No, he couldn't believe she was the killer. But there remained the gold coin. And now, no one would take her word that Bent had given it to her. And if they did, then she would be accused of the murder. Talk about a tangle.

He shook his head. "I don't know what else you could have done either," he finally replied. "Just don't say anything about our talk here. It'll be our secret. I've got some other places to look."

A happy grin jumped on her face. "You

mean, you believe me?"

His reply erased the smile from her lips. "I don't know. All I know is that Bent didn't kill Bledsoe. You might have had a reason, and you might have done it." He paused, then added, "I don't know what to think except I still got me a heap more looking around to do."

Their eyes met, and Slade saw the hurt in hers before she turned and walked away.

As Slade watched Sarah Cook disappear into the dusk, he tried to sort the confused thoughts tumbling through his head. He didn't want to believe that she had killed Bledsoe, but one fact kept coming back to nag at him, one that provided Sarah Cook motive enough. Wiley Bledsoe had a large stash of money hidden in the lard bucket, more than enough to carry the young woman far from New Gideon and give her time and the wherewithal to begin a new life for herself.

But then, if she had murdered Bledsoe, why didn't she take the money? Or did Wiley Bledsoe have even more loot hidden away than that which Slade had discovered? Sarah Cook was bright, bright enough to take what she wanted and leave enough behind to cast off any suspicion.

That same nagging worry came back to

bother him again. He closed his eyes, trying to make the vaporous idea solidify, but it continued to evade his grasp.

CHAPTER EIGHT

Bent looked up from his plate of fried pork, steamed peas, oven biscuits, and cream gravy when Slade, hungry as a new thrown calf, came in. Bent's cheeks bulged with a mouthful of Mrs. Ware's mouth-watering, stomach-stretching spread. All the older man could do was nod.

Slade grinned and cast a quick glance at Joseph Ware. He was concerned that the big blacksmith might question the young man's whereabouts that evening, and Slade did not want to reveal any of his conversation with Sarah Cook — not even the fact they had spoken.

He need not have worried for Ware had other things on his mind. "I'm sure glad you're back," he said hurriedly. "We got problems, big problems."

With an effort, Bent managed to gulp down his mouthful of chuck and shake his head. "I told Joseph that it was all just wild palavering, nothing else."

"What's he talking about?" Slade asked the blacksmith.

"We had some visitors today. Garth Smith was doing the talking, but if I was a gambling man, I'd wager my stocking bay that his father put him up to it."

"Up to what?"

Ware gestured to Bent who continued putting himself around the big meal on the table, exhibiting no concern over their visitors. "Some of our *leaders* have decided that two weeks would be time enough for you to find the killer, so they went ahead and put in a call for the circuit judge."

The muscles in Slade's jaw twitched as he considered the implications of Ware's announcement. He fixed his eyes on Bent who had pushed his empty plate aside and leaned back in his chair and patted his full stomach, contented. "You sure don't seem worried," the young half-breed snapped, irritated by the older man's seeming indifference.

Bent grinned. "That's because I got faith in you."

Slade plopped down at the table and politely declined the plate offered him by Mrs. Ware, settling instead for a tall glass of cold water straight from the well. The hunger in his stomach had disappeared.

Ware leaned forward. "Did you find any-thing?"

The young half-breed shook his head. "There's sign to the north. I put Nana on it. I'm to meet him out on the prairie tomor-row."

"Think he'll find them for us?" Ware frowned.

Bent snorted at the blacksmith. "That In-jun can find 'em if anyone can. Why, I see'd him track a cockroach across a mountain one time."

Slade suppressed a grin as the black-smith's face clouded with disbelief. The large man glanced at Slade and saw the laughter in the younger man's eyes. He turned back to Bent. "That is very hard to believe, Mr. Bent."

Bent held up his hand, palm open and forward. "It's the gospel. I —" He paused, realizing what he had said. Under his grizzled beard, his face colored. "Well, maybe not the gospel, but close enough to make me feel good about him finding them rustlers."

Slade, lost in his own thoughts, sipped at the glass of water while Bent regaled the blacksmith with stories of Nana's tracking ability. He knew how capable a tracker his

Apache brother was, but there were times when even the best tracker ran into a blind trail.

The next morning, Slade rode out of New Gideon before sunrise. The sun was directly overhead when he reined up on top of a sagebrush-covered sand hill. He removed his slouch hat and wiped the sweat from his forehead with his shirtsleeve. He scanned the vast and empty prairie surrounding him. A blanket of wiry shortgrass covered the rolling sand hills that were dotted with oak shinnery and purple sage.

After nooning in a patch of shinnery, a cluster of tough oaks wrist thick and head high, Slade tightened the cinch on the blue roan and continued north. Somewhere ahead, Nana waited.

Midafternoon, Slade left the rolling sand hills and topped out on the Staked Plains, thousands of square miles flatter than even a wet leaf.

Late afternoon, a dark line appeared on the horizon. Near dusk, as Slade grew closer, the line turned green. He grunted with satisfaction. At least he wouldn't camp dry tonight.

The twisting line of cottonwoods and elm began taking shape. Soon Slade saw a thin wisp of white smoke curling from the leafy canopy of green lining the river. He reined up.

For several minutes, Slade studied the river, his ears tuned for any unusual sound. All seemed normal. To his left above the trees, a tiny swallow darted and swooped as it nagged at a crow. Off to his right, two cottontails nibbled idly at a patch of short-grass. A gray squirrel paused on the trunk of a large cottonwood to stare at Slade, then with a rapid *kuk kuk kuk,* skittered behind the trunk.

The young half-breed knew then that whoever built the fire was no greener. He had come in, made his camp, and cooked a meal, all without spooking the animals. With a click of his tongue, he eased the roan forward, at the same time slipping the rawhide loop off the hammer of his .44. He then rested his hand on his thigh as he rode into the grove of trees.

The sharp smell of wood smoke filled the grove. His gray eyes quartered through the cottonwoods and elm. Beyond the trees, the river rolled and eddied. To his left, a tiny fire in the middle of a clearing twinkled in the growing dusk. He halted. No one was around. No horse, no gear, nothing.

He rode closer, his hand resting on the

butt of his .44. Behind him, the squirrel chattered, a slower *kuk kuk kuk* to indicate that the danger had passed. Slade glanced over his shoulder. The squirrel perched on a limb staring at him, its tail curled against its back, a sure sign that all was well.

Slade reined, staring down at the half-dozen fillets of fish on spits around the fire.

Suddenly, a whippoorwill called. Slade listened carefully. A grin burst over his dark face when he heard the coo of a dove. Nana!

In the same instant, Nana appeared from behind a cottonwood, his broad grin a white streak against his dark face. He gestured to the fish. "Busca is always hungry."

"As the badger," Slade replied, dismounting. "But first, what luck did you have?"

"Good. The men you seek are to the north, two days for the white man, one for the Indian," he added with a taunting grin on his face. "Come. Eat, and I will tell you of what I found."

Slade ignored Nana's good-natured attempt to bait him. "Shoot."

With a shrug, Nana quickly related the details of his journey while they ate.

A frown knit Slade's brow when Nana told him of the ranch that wasn't a ranch. "I don't understand."

Nana gave a crooked grin. "The men are

not wranglers. The one who owns the ranch does not fool me. The white man cannot match the Apache at trickery. He wishes outsiders to believe his is a working ranch, but it is not."

"You mean," asked Slade, his hopes ballooning once again. "The ranch is just a way to hide the rustling?"

"The men spend their days in the bunkhouse. They play cards and drink white man's whiskey. And there is no cattle. What am I to think?"

Slade considered Nana's words for several seconds. Then he asked. "Can you slip in and take one of the men without being seen?"

A smug grin broke Nana's usually emotionless face. "Does the north wind bring cold?"

With a wry grin, Slade nodded. "Here's what I want you to do."

CHAPTER NINE

The young rustler slowly opened his eyes against the throbbing in his skull. He lay on his back, staring up at the glow of firelight dancing on the overhead leaves. He tried to roll over, but something held him. He turned his head, and sudden fear coursed through his body. He jerked his head around to stare at his other wrist. He was spread-eagled, wet rawhide lashing his wrists to stakes driven into the ground. He tried to move his legs, but they were also bound tightly.

Wood smoke stung his nostrils. He jerked his head in the direction of the smoke, straining to lift his body so he could see the fire. A sob tore from his throat when he saw the Indian squatting by the fire.

At the man's whimper, the Indian looked up, and a sneer curled his lips as he rose and slipped his knife from its sheath. He stared down at the struggling young man.

Slowly, the Indian squatted and poked the tip of the blade against the taut skin under the bound man's chin. With tantalizing deliberation, he nudged the point of the double-edged blade down the young man's throat, brushed over his sternum, teased across his belly, and paused at his waist. The savage's sneer broadened as he increased pressure on his knife. The gleaming blade depressed the taut flesh, but not enough to cut.

The young rustler caught his breath when he saw the muscles on the Indian's arms tense in preparation for a slashing cut.

Abruptly, the Indian's face contorted and a chilling scream ripped from his throat. He jerked the knife above his head.

The young rustler tried to scream, but the words clogged in his throat as his eyes fixed on the orange flames reflecting off the shiny blade. In the middle of the young rustler's terror, the roar of a six-gun echoed through the night, slamming the Indian to the ground.

The terrified young man jerked his head in the direction of the gunfire and saw a lanky man, gun in hand, standing in the stirrups astride a big roan that was thundering down on him from out of the darkness. A second roar filled the night and orange fire erupted from the muzzle of the man's gun. The Indian's limp body jerked.

Shaking with relief, the young rustler watched as the man dismounted and rolled the Indian over with the toe of his moccasin. The stranger studied the motionless Indian for several seconds before pulling out his own knife and quickly slashing the rustler's bonds.

"Hells bells, mister," said the young man in a shaky voice, rising to his feet quickly and brushing the dust from his denims. "I never been so glad to see a body in my life." He offered his hand. "Name's Joe Rearden. I — I —" He hesitated while he tried to still the quiver in his voice. "I'm damned grateful to you."

Slade took Rearden's hand, noting that the pale-faced man was only a boy — seventeen, maybe eighteen. "You must've done something powerful mean to make that brave want to carve you up."

Rearden shuddered as he stared at the still body. Two dark blotches stained the Indian's vest. "I never seen that redstick before. All I know is that I went outside the bunkhouse during the night, and the next thing I know, I'm laying here tied fitter than Cooter's mare." He reached for the knife in his boot. "I figure the boys are gonna hurrah me when I git back to the ranch, so I reckon I'll just git me a scalp and put the squelch on some of their yowlings."

"No," said Slade, laying his hand on the boy's arm.

Rearden looked around, puzzled. "What are you talking about? This redstick was gonna kill me."

"Forget the hurrahing. I'll go back with you and testify that you took care of business here. The worst thing you can do to that Injun is leave his scalp alone."

The boy stared at Slade uncertainly.

Slade continued. "This one's Apache. When they die, they want to be scalped. That's their way of getting to the other world. It's a sign of bravery."

A puzzled frown on his face, Joe Rearden grunted. "I never heard that before."

With a nonchalant shrug of his shoulders, Slade said. "Apache is back in Arizona Territory. I suspect they got different beliefs than the Comanche and Kiowa around here." He paused, then added casually. "Wonder what this one was doing so far from his rancheria."

He could see the wheels turning in Joe Rearden's head as the young boy pondered Slade's words. Slade decided not to give Rearden a chance to consider further. Nodding to the spavined sorrel standing hipshot nearby, he said, "Get the sorrel. Let's go." He swung into the saddle, and with a click of his tongue, Slade deliberately turned the roan downriver.

Rearden stopped him. "Hey. That's the wrong way. We go upriver," he said, climbing onto the sorrel.

Slade nodded and wheeled his pony about. Rearden had already moved out.

As soon as Rearden was out of earshot, Slade stopped and stared down at the Indian sprawled on the ground. "I reckon you're a fair playactor," he whispered.

Nana opened his eyes and grinned up at his brother.

During the ride to the ranch, Slade glimpsed a figure darker than the night following them. He smiled with satisfaction, wondering if white brothers were as loyal and faithful as his Apache brother. He found such a concept difficult to believe.

Though he himself was half-white, Slade was just as faithful to Nana and to Paleto as they to him. He had always believed the fierce family loyalty the three shared was a result of the Indian blood coursing through his veins. Maybe white families were just as loyal, he told himself. Hard to say. He'd never had any experience with white families other than Three-Fingers Bent. But he didn't think so.

He glanced up at the great bear in the northern sky, what the white man called the Big Dipper. His eyes settled on the three stars that formed the tail of the bear, and recollected how as youths, he and Nana and their brother, Paleto, swore they would always be as close and as enduring as the three stars.

An hour after sunrise, the young rustler interrupted Slade's thoughts. "There it is, yonder in that stretch of elms."

Slade looked in the direction Rearden pointed, surprised to have reached the ranch without warning. During the last two hours on the vast prairie, he had seen no cattle.

Nana's judgment appeared sound. This spread didn't look like a working ranch. Not even a greasy sack herd to be seen.

Slade's gray eyes narrowed as they searched the prairie around him. He'd never seen a ranch without an overabundance of cow pies ready to be stepped in or over. Although the horse biscuits were fresh, what cow patties he saw were dry, ready to fall apart at the slightest touch. That meant the ranch hadn't seen beef for a few weeks.

Perhaps he would soon have some answers to the questions raised by Wiley Bledsoe's death.

"Don't forget what you said back there, about me taking care of the redstick."

Slade grunted. "I won't." He turned his eyes on the ranch house.

The main house was whitewashed lap-strake with a covered porch spanning the front. Behind the main house sat a weathered bunkhouse, its windows and doors filled with curious men watching the approaching riders. A short distance behind the bunkhouse was a gabled barn with a cluster of corrals constructed of sawn timbers fastened with thick spikes of iron.

Joe Rearden pulled up in front of the main house. The door opened and a tall man with a white beard and wearing a black suit stepped onto the porch. Rearden nodded. "I'm back, Mr. Daughtery. Don't know why, but three redsticks carried me off last night. Soon as I got loose, I damned well sent ever' one of them to meet their Maker."

John Daughtery's broad forehead wrinkled as he arched a skeptical eyebrow, his eyes dropping to Rearden's empty holster. "Quite a trick, Joe-Boy," he said in a voice which surprised Slade because of its obvious culture.

"It's the truth, Mr. Daughtery. This jasper here can vouch for me. He done seen me do it."

Daughtery looked at Slade. Slade shrugged. "I can't vouch for the other two, but I reckon I did see one dead Injun."

Rearden's beardless cheeks glowed with satisfaction but Daughtery ignored the boy as he studied Slade, his sharp eyes pausing momentarily on Slade's moccasined feet. "You from around here, stranger?" His eyes flicked up to the war club on Slade's hip.

"Nope. Never been in this part of the state. Don't intend on staying either."

Stroking his full-cut white beard, Daughtery took in Slade's lank, wiry figure with slumped shoulders, sunken chest, legs resting easily on the roan's ribs. But when he looked deeper, he saw a blazing intensity in the young man's gray eyes. A chill ran up his back. John Daughtery had the strange feeling that he was staring at a keg of black powder with a lit fuse.

He glanced at Rearden. "Go on to the bunkhouse, Joe-Boy. I'd like to visit a spell with Mr. —" He hesitated. "I didn't get your handle, mister."

"Didn't give it, but that's no matter. Name's Slade, Jake Slade from Arizona Territory."

"Come on in the house, Mr. Slade," said Daughtery, turning and leading the way inside. "It's early, but I figure that prairie dust has given you a powerful thirst."

Slade followed the tall man inside, aware of the stares in his direction. He paused inside the door to accustom his eyes to the shadows.

Daughtery poured two drinks from a cut glass decanter and handed one to Slade. "Now suppose you tell me what really happened out there, Mr. Slade. Joe-Boy is still wet behind the ears. There's no way he could have handled even one Kiowa, let alone three."

The young half-breed sipped his whiskey. Bourbon. Good bourbon, too. Not the molasses sweetened bile sold by Indian traders. "Why don't you ask him, Mr. Daughtery? He seems a right agreeable waddy."

"He is, Mr. Slade. He is. To be perfectly honest, I didn't want to embarrass him. Way I figure it is that he found himself in a peck of trouble, and you come along and bailed him out. That right?"

A slight grin curled one side of Slade's lips. "Could be."

Daughtery laughed. "I figured as much. How many Kiowas was it?"

"One. An Apache."

A frown wrinkled Daughtery's forehead. "I don't ever remember hearing of Apaches around here."

Slade did not reply.

Daughtery continued. "Why did he take Joe-Boy?"

"Who knows what makes Injuns do what they do? Somebody must've jiggled God's arm when He poured brains in the Apache."

Daughtery laughed again. "As good a reason as I ever heard, Mr. Slade." The laughter faded from his eyes. "Now that brings us to you."

Slade hid the sudden tension filling his body. This was the moment he had waited for. "I don't see I have nothing to do with anything," he replied, deliberately testy.

The older man grinned. "Forgive me. I'm not prying. Just curious why you rode in here with Joe-Boy."

Relaxing, Slade replied. "Well, I could say he seemed too innocent to be left out there by himself. But the truth is, I figured I might latch on to a few days' work for some grub." He glanced out the window and said. "But, it don't look like you need any hands. You don't have work enough for those you got now."

Slade's frank appraisal of the ranch's situation caught Daughtery by surprise. He replied, too hastily, "Just a slow period, Mr. Slade, but I am obliged for the help you gave Joe-Boy. You're more'n welcome to hang around a day or two and rest up your animal."

It was Slade's turn to be surprised. He had expected more than an invitation for a few days. He turned up the glass and drained it. "Thanks, but I'll mosey on. Maybe on up to Fort Dodge. I hear there's work up there."

"Not much. Most of it no better than saloon swamping from what I hear."

Slade shrugged. "Some of us can't be too particular. Work is work." He set the glass on the table and turned to the door. He hoped that Daughtery would get the message.

"Wait a minute, Mr. Slade. Maybe we can work something out."

Slade's pulse raced. "Such as?" He turned to face Daughtery.

John Daughtery eyed Slade for several seconds, trying to determine if his first impression was right. "Tell you what. See Ed Towers in the bunkhouse. Send him to me and tell him you're on the books for thirty a month and found. We got some stock coming in a couple days." He glanced at the moccasins on the young half-breed's feet. "I got a feel you're damned good with horses. I can always use a jasper who knows horses."

Slade nodded, maintaining an impassive face. "I'm not looking for handouts, Mr. Daughtery."

Daughtery grinned. "Believe me, Mr. Slade. This will be no handout. When we get that stock in, you'll be polishing the saddle eighteen — twenty hours a day."

Touching his fingers to the brim on his slouch hat in a salute, Slade said, "That being the case, I'm much obliged to you, Mr. Daughtery."

CHAPTER TEN

Ed Towers was a hulking brute with massive shoulders and a perpetual sneer on his thick lips. His breath reeked of cheap whiskey, and spiderwebs of red covered the whites of his eyes.

When Slade relayed Daughtery's message, Towers snorted and stomped out of the bunkhouse toward the main house, the star-shaped rowels on his spurs jangling.

Young Joe Rearden sidled up to Slade. "The bunk next to mine is empty. You can throw your bedroll there."

Slade didn't move. He surveyed the bunkhouse while his eyes grew accustomed to the dark. Half a dozen surly men stared back at him, their dislike obvious.

Ignoring their hostile stares, Slade tossed his bedroll on the bunk and went out to take care of his horse. Joe Rearden tagged after him, pointing out the well, the corrals, the cook shack, even the three-hole outhouse.

Slade was so absorbed in studying the ranch that Rearden's words passed in one ear and out the other. His first impression had been right. This was no working ranch. The outlying corrals were empty, although there was old sign that they had been filled within the past weeks. A dozen horses milled about in the corral behind the barn.

Inside the barn, Slade unsaddled the roan and turned it out with the others. He watched through the open door as the animal dashed into the corral, then slid to a halt, its reddish brown eyes fastened on a piebald stallion that had taken a step toward the newcomer. For a moment, the two animals stared at each other, then the roan trotted around the piebald and stopped at the water trough.

"Looks like your animal's afraid of the piebald. That's Ed's horse," said Rearden, trying to make conversation.

"Looks that way," replied Slade laconically. "But I wouldn't ever count on the way a thing looks."

Joe Rearden looked up at Slade whose eyes remained on the roan. "You saying your animal could whip up on the pie?"

Slade turned to the younger man. "Nope. I'm just saying don't be fooled by what you think you see." He paused and gestured to

105

the empty prairie behind the corral. "Like this ranch."

"What about it?"

"It looks like a ranch, but every ranch I saw was filled with bawling calves and bellowing mamas being cussed by yelling cowpokes. I don't know what this place is, but it's no ranch."

Rearden's face blanched. He glanced over his shoulder and shuddered with relief when he saw no one was in the barn with them. He touched his finger to his lips to silence Slade. "Don't talk like that," he said in an alarmed whisper. "Someone might be listening."

Before Slade could reply, the barn door swung open and two figures stood silhouetted by the setting sun, one tall and slender, the other shorter and thickset — John Daughtery and Ed Towers.

Daughtery waved him over. "Ed and I talked it all over, and we both agree we can use you."

One look at the suppressed anger burning Ed Towers' cheeks told Slade that Daughtery was lying. The massive man glared malevolently at Slade as Daughtery continued. "My primary job is dealing with animals on consignment. I can use you if you meant what you said about not being particular. If you are a particular individual, you best saddle up and ride out." Daughtery grinned, but the threat in his words chilled Slade's blood.

He paused to give Slade time to consider.

"I'm not particular," Slade replied, filled with the overpowering feeling that had he tried to ride away, he would never have reached the barn door.

Towers grunted. Daughtery continued. "I have a party up in the Indian Territory that's in the market for good horses. We're leaving in the morning to pick up the animals for delivery."

"Sounds fine to me. Where do I fit in?"

"I'll tell you when the time is right. Now, cook's got steaks and beans on the fire. Fill your belly and then hit the blankets. Four o'clock comes early."

Slade elbowed Joe Rearden. "You heard the man. Let's us put ourselves around those steaks."

As Slade and Rearden left the barn, Ed Towers hissed at his boss, "You got feathers for brains. You don't know nothing about that half-breed."

Daughtery's eyes narrowed. "The episode about Joe puzzles me. I want this hombre around until I'm satisfied. Still, I think he'll make us a good hand, but just in case, keep

107

your eyes on him. First wrong move, blow his damned head off."

Towers patted the black-handled revolver on his hip. "The sooner the better," he sneered. "I don't like Injuns noway, but there's something extra about that jasper that itches at me."

The foreman's words erased Daughtery's concern. He knew from experience that from this moment on, every move Slade made would be scrutinized by the hulking foreman, and that if the younger man took even one false step, it would be his last.

That night when Towers returned to the bunkhouse, Slade's eyes were closed, and his breathing was regular. Moonlight flooding through the open window bathed the half-breed's angular face.

The foreman stared from the darkness at the sleeping man, his slow-moving brain trying to sort the feelings that had left him so perplexed and frightened over Jake Slade. Finally, unable to draw up the reason he was so confused, the heavily muscled man dropped into his bunk without bothering to undress.

When Ed Towers finally dozed, Slade's eyes popped open. A grim smile played over his lips before he went to sleep.

At four o'clock, the men rose, put themselves around leftover beans and fresh coffee and mounted up. By the time the sun rose, the ranch lay ten miles behind. All day Daughtery led the party in a walking run to the east. All day, Slade kept his ears tuned to every whispered conversation, but no mention of Wiley Bledsoe or the Mormon community of New Gideon was made.

The packed earth of the Staked Plains began to give way to sand as the terrain gently inclined into the rolling hills of Indian Territory. By midafternoon, Slade guessed they were due north of New Gideon by about thirty or forty miles. If any of the rustlers were aware of the fact, they said nothing. He glanced over his shoulder. Somewhere out there, Nana trailed the party, waiting for the right time to contact Slade.

They reached their destination at midnight. Daughtery reined up. "Cold camp, boys. There's a small creek back west a piece, but stay inside the hills around us. In the morning, you'll see what we're after."

Feeling eyes on his every move, Slade did as he was told.

Next morning, Daughtery took them to the crest of a sandhill. To the east, the territory dropped away in a great, sweeping valley over twenty miles in length. In the middle of the valley clustered a collection of buildings. Beyond the buildings, animals grazed.

"There it is, boys," drawled John Daughtery. "Fort Sherman. There's five hundred head of choice horses down there, and we got a couple Kiowa chiefs back east a piece that'll buy every last one of them with gold, not greenbacks."

A gleeful mutter arose. Daughtery continued. "The corrals are on the far side of the fort." His dark eyes found Slade's and held them in a vise. "Like before, we'll ride in and drive the animals south a few miles before making a sweep to the east." Daughtery broke his gaze and surveyed the other men. "We'll rest up here today and hit them tonight after midnight. There's a late moon so we won't have any trouble," the rustler leader added.

Towers grunted and glanced at Slade.

Slade knew he was being watched. He figured the smartest play for him was to do nothing, just go along and see what happened. The army could afford to lose some stock.

The remainder of the day was uneventful. Slade took secret delight in seeing the frustration grow in Ed Towers. The big man's eyes never left Slade as the young half-breed, his hat over his face, lay in the shade of a willow on a low knoll overlooking a small stream bubbling from the rocks and winding its way down into the valley. But Slade did not sleep. He listened, but learned nothing. With each passing minute Slade made no suspicious move, Towers' frustration grew.

Late in the afternoon when Towers and Daughtery had their heads together over some last minute changes, Slade eased downstream and flopped on his belly to drink from the icy cold creek. A faint sound in the underbrush across the stream froze him. He resumed drinking, but his eyes searched the thick foliage from beneath his eyebrows. Though he could not see him, Slade knew that Nana was watching.

"Is it you?"

Nana's familiar voice answered. "Yes."

"I haven't much time. Listen hard. Tonight, we take horses from the fort. We —"

At that moment, Towers' raucous voice sounded from the knoll. "Slade! Where in the hell are you?"

Rising to his feet and dragging his shirtsleeve across his lips, Slade whispered across the stream. "The horses at the fort. Tonight." He raised his voice. "Over here! What's up?"

Spurs jangling, Towers stomped down the knoll. "What'n the hell you doin' down here?" His thick hand resting on his revolver, he glared at Slade.

Slade grinned. "Man gets thirsty, Ed. What's eating you? You act like you got a boot full of ants."

The hulking man's nostrils flared in anger. Someone behind the foreman snickered. He spun around. Several of the men were watching, amused expressions on their faces. When Towers turned back around, Slade had returned to his spot under the willow. Incensed, the foreman stomped away.

Just before midnight, the rustlers mounted and headed toward the fort, a collection of clapboard buildings arranged in a square facing a quadrangle, which was also used as a parade grounds. Just to the south of the fort sprawled the corrals.

Lights twinkled in the fort, reminding Slade of the lightning bugs that filled the night when he was a boy. A smaller light flared, a match marking the position of a sentry.

Soon Daughtery pulled up. He gave his commands in a hushed, terse voice. The lack of explanation told Slade that this was a job that had been done many times before.

"And you, Slade, you ride with Towers."

With a nod, Slade reined his roan back alongside the hulking foreman. Joe Rearden and a fence post of a man named José Segura dropped into drag. Slowly, the band began spreading until Daughtery and his lead men, now only darker shadows in the star-filled night, rode a hundred yards ahead of Slade and Towers.

The plan was simple and easily executed. Daughtery and his lead men would burst in on the sentries, throw open the gates as the next wave of rustlers, including Slade and Towers, dashed in at full gallop, spooking the horses. That set the stage for the last wave to ride in and mop up on the sentries before the surprised soldiers had a chance to gather their thoughts.

The thunder of hoofbeats sounded ahead. Towers growled. "Now, dammit, dig them spurs in."

Within half a dozen steps, Slade's blue roan was at a full gallop. Ahead, Daughtery appeared as only a nebulous shadow.

Just as Daughtery threw open the gate, the crack of a single rifle broke the silence.

From the darkness beyond the fence, an angry voice cried out, "Hold your fire, dammit. Not yet."

But the nervous and excited soldiers ignored the command. A fusillade of gunfire exploded from the darkness in an unending chain of orange muzzle blasts. Slugs whistled through the air, slamming into the army mounts milling in the open gate. Frightened horses squealed and whinnied.

By then, Slade and Towers had reached the corral. Startled, Towers jerked his piebald around, slamming it into Slade's roan. For a moment, the two horses fought against each other.

"Get the hell outta my way," yelled Towers, slashing his spurs into his mount's flanks.

"Not without the horses," Slade yelled back. He knew that although the ambush was a result of the information he had given Nana, he himself, at this time, was just another rustler to the soldiers.

Towers hesitated.

Slade led the way. "Follow me."

The night was a cacophony of sound and sight, stark blackness ravished by orange and red muzzle blasts. Springfields boomed. Colts cracked. Men cursed. Horses bawled. Dust rose in suffocating clouds from the torn ground.

Leaning low over the roan's neck to avoid the humming slugs, Slade drove the animal into the milling horses. The frightened animals had no direction. If he could drive the lead animals from the gate, the others would follow. Above the confusion, he heard Towers' muttered curses behind him.

The starlight dimly silhouetted the horses. As Slade pushed through the kicking and pawing animals, a white horse reared, its front hooves clawing the air in fear.

Knowing the roan would follow, Slade lightly leaped onto the white horse's back and clamped his legs around the animal's ribs as he grabbed a handful of mane. Before the startled animal could react, Slade slammed his heels into the white's flanks and sent the powerful stallion leaping into the darkness away from the ambush.

The thunder of hoofbeats behind him told Slade his plan had worked. Other horses pulled up beside him. Two or three moved ahead, and suddenly, with a startled squeal, two crowhopped back in Slade's path as the third crashed to the ground.

The white swerved, and as Slade swept past the fallen horse, he saw the pole fence the soldiers had built to contain the rustlers.

By now, every light in the post was lit. If fences had been erected on one side of the fort, chances were they were all around. The only way out for Slade and the rustlers was the way they had come in.

Twisting his fingers into the horse's mane and digging a heel under the point of the hip, Slade slid onto the horse's side, Indian style. The stampeding horses cut through the middle of the post amid racketing rifle fire and shouting men.

Seconds later, the galloping herd burst into the night, and Slade pulled himself upright on the horse's back, at the same time keeping the white in a full gallop. He had no way of knowing how many of the rustlers were following, but he had no intention of waiting around to find out.

Slade kept the white stallion in full stride until the lights from the post faded into the night. Only then did he ease up. Glancing over his shoulder, he saw the roan dutifully following at the head of about fifty wild-eyed horses. He whistled, and the roan moved up. Slade changed horses.

Daughtery finally caught up with him and motioned to the left. Slade fell in behind as they drove the herd across the valley up onto the flats of the Staked Plains.

An hour later, they stopped to breathe the animals at a tiny creek. Four other rustlers brought up the rear, Joe Rearden among them. As the four quieted the nervous horses, Daughtery pulled up beside Slade.

116

"Figured you knew horses, but not like that," he said, a new respect in his voice.

"Grew up with them."

Seconds passed as the two men stared into the darkness that filled each other's faces. John Daughtery shook his head and looked over their back trail. There was amusement in his voice. "Well, it looks like we might have left a few horses scattered across the valley."

Slade grinned. "More than a few. I reckon we're lucky to get what we got." He paused and looked around. "What about the other boys?"

Daughtery shrugged. "They'll be along directly. They been through this sort of thing before."

Hoping to thrust aside any suspicion, Slade muttered, "Those army boys looked like they was waiting for us."

With a shake of his head, Daughtery grunted. "It does at that, doesn't it?"

Sure enough, Towers and Segura caught them at nooning the next day. Towers glared at Slade, who was squatting by the small fire. Regardless of how bad the situation had been, the hulking foreman disliked anyone taking the lead. He doubly hated the half-breed for being the one.

"We're still missing one man," Slade said to Daughtery, his eyes on Ed Towers.

The remark was innocent enough, but it slapped Ed Towers in the face.

Daughtery glanced across the fire at Slade, then looked up at Towers who replied, "Wes didn't make it out of the post. We was riding together when he got knocked out of the saddle." The big foreman looked over the meager herd. "Not much for what we went through."

Daughtery rose to his feet and dusted off his denims. "It happens, Ed," he replied casually, too casually Slade thought. "I guess we'd better hit the trail. Those soldier boys are out there looking for us."

Towers fixed Slade with a crazed look. "Them soldier boys knew we was coming."

Daughtery grunted. "Slade said the same thing, Ed. Well, don't fret. We'll have time to get to the bottom of it back at the ranch. I've got a couple hunches and I want to see how they play out. Now, let's ride."

Slade turned to his roan and hooked the stirrup over the saddle horn to tighten the cinch. He heard Towers reply, "It didn't hafta happen. We shoulda had an insider there like we do with them Mormons."

"Shut up, Ed," hissed Daughtery.

A tingle ran down Slade's spine, but he

tightened the cinch without hesitation, giving no indication of having overheard the exchange. He mounted and turned an unassuming face to John Daughtery. "Let's move 'em."

CHAPTER ELEVEN

After selling the horses to the Kiowa chiefs, Kicking Bird and Big Tree, the small band of rustlers headed southwest. The ride to the ranch was uneventful. Slade kept his ears cocked for any further mention of the Mormons, but nothing more was said of New Gideon.

"Now what?" Slade glanced at Daughtery as they unsaddled their own horses in the barn and turned them loose to graze.

"Come inside and see," the rustler leader replied, nodding to the main house.

Slade followed, wary of the next few minutes.

Once inside the parlor, Daughtery opened a cherrywood sideboard and returned with three glasses and a bottle of Cyrus Noble whiskey. He filled the three glasses. "Have one. Ed'll be in soon."

With a wry grin, Slade plopped in a satin wing chair and nodded. "Thanks, but I got a feeling Ed won't be too taken with me being here."

Daughtery's black eyes glittered in amusement. "Well, I got me a feeling that won't make much difference to a man like you." He held up his glass in a toast.

Slade returned the gesture as a knock sounded at the door. Without taking his eyes off Slade, Daughtery said, "Come on in, Ed."

Towers entered and jerked to an abrupt halt, staring at the young half-breed slouched in the fancy wingback chair, wearing a smug grin. The foreman cut his eyes to John Daughtery. "What's he doin' here?"

The tall rancher nodded to the table. "Have a drink, Ed. The three of us are going to reach an understanding."

Reluctantly, Towers picked up a glass.

"Sit down, Ed."

For several seconds, Ed Towers stared at John Daughtery before finally acceding to the older man's request.

Daughtery glanced at Slade who continued to wear a wry grin. The rancher suppressed a smile. Damn him, the rancher thought to himself with amusement. He damn well knows just how much that grin infuriates Towers.

Slade was Daughtery's kind of man, and

he wasn't about to let a thin-skinned hired hand like Ed Towers run the younger man off. He decided to get right to the point.

"To your health, gentlemen," said Daughtery, taking a sip of whiskey.

Slade dipped his glass to each man, but Ed Towers refused to drink.

Daughtery ignored the slight. Ed Towers had the disposition of a rabid dog, but in a fight, whether a barroom free-for-all, a back alley brawl, or a face-to-face gunfight, he had few equals. As far as John Daughtery was concerned, the one quality offset the other. But now was another matter. He cleared his throat.

The rancher fixed his eyes on Towers. "Ed, I don't know what your problem is with Slade, but you either forget it or light a shuck out of here. Slade proved himself back at the post while the rest of us went in circles like a dog chasing his tail. We got out of there with a whole hide because of him, pure and simple."

The foreman's ears burned, and his fingers whitened around the glass.

Daughtery continued. "I figure Slade here to be a special man just like you're special in your own way." The rancher's voice grew cold and unrelenting. "I'm taking him in, Ed, and I don't want any trouble from you about it."

Towers glared at Slade.

The young half-breed remained slouched in the wingback, but his muscles tensed as he watched the range of emotions from murderous hatred to resigned acquiescence contort the burly foreman's face. With a grunt, Towers turned up his glass and drained it. Only then did Slade relax.

With a satisfied nod, John Daughtery said. "We won't have time to relax much. In a day or two, we'll pull out for New Gideon."

To keep the excitement from showing on his face, Slade took a drink of whiskey.

Towers asked, "Bledsoe send word?"

Daughtery shook his head. "Haven't heard from him in a couple weeks."

"What if we don't hear from him? I ain't never trusted him no more'n a coyote in the chicken house."

"He's been right in the past, but to be on the safe side, I sent out a man before we struck out for Fort Sherman." Daughtery glanced at Slade.

Sensing that it was time for him to leave, the young half-breed rose and drained his glass. "If you fellers don't need me, I'm ready to hit the soogans. I'm plumb beat."

"Take the bottle with you," Daughtery said affably.

"No, thanks. One's my limit."

After Slade closed the door, Daughtery turned to Towers. "Ed, there's something I want to talk over with you." He cut his eyes toward the door Slade had just closed.

That night, Slade tried to fit the pieces into the puzzle. His guess about Bledsoe had been right.

The dead man had been one of the rustlers. During his infrequent but lengthy disappearances, he rode with John Daughtery and his gang. That accounted for the expensive appointments and clothes in his Spartan house as well as the cash in the lard pail beneath the puncheon floor.

Don't worry, Bent. I'll have you out of there real soon, he said to himself.

The next day, the men lazed around, patching their gear and each trying to tell bigger lies than the man before. Camaraderie filled the bunkhouse with good-natured joking and impish pranks. Several of the men now directed questions to Slade, for his quick thinking back at the fort had broken down the animosity the men had held toward him. He was part of the gang now, one of the boys, and Joe Rearden tagged after him like a friendly puppy.

Slade had taken a liking to the young boy. At first, he thought it was because he felt guilty about duping Joe Rearden and using the young boy's gratitude to secure himself a place in the gang. After a couple days, Slade had realized that he did indeed enjoy the boy's company and desperately wished for some way to sidetrack him from the owl-hoot trail without jeopardizing his own furtive infiltration of the gang. He had never known a rustler to die rich. They all ended up the same way, at the end of a rope or moldering away out on the prairie, carrion for coyotes and buzzards and fertilizer for the grass.

The next afternoon while Slade was sitting in the shade of the bunkhouse mending his reins, he glanced out of the corners of his eyes at Joe Rearden who sat next to him. Joe had been jabbering about the ranch land up north in Wyoming and Montana, and had reckoned that once he saved the money, he would buy himself a nice little spread. "I heard tell that a man could pick up a few thousand acres at a decent price."

"Man could do a lot worse," Slade said. Using his double-edged knife, he drilled a hole in either end of the broken rein and began splicing them with rawhide. "You planning on taking a wife with you?"

The young boy blushed and ducked his head. "Naw. Don't have no one in mind. It'll just be me and Ma. At least, at the beginning. Then maybe later on . . ." His voice faded away.

Hoofbeats interrupted them. Slade looked around. Two riders stopped at the ranch house and entered without knocking. Rearden nodded at the duo. "That's Kansas Jack. I don't know the other gent. I met Jack up at Daughtery's other place."

"Other place?"

Rearden nodded. "Yep. Mr. Daughtery's got a spread about thirty or forty miles northeast of here. I only been there onct, but like I said, that's where I met Jack."

Slade pursed his lips, but said nothing. The one named Kansas Jack looked familiar.

Rearden continued. "Word is Daughtery sent Jack to El Paso. I don't know what for."

Suddenly Slade realized why the man seemed familiar. He was the grubliner who had come into Slade's camp out on the Staked Plains, the one who had been so surprised to see two white men squatting around a fire with an Apache.

Slade muttered an oath under his breath as his brain raced, feverishly searching for options. By just showing up, that owlhoot had just thrown a wide loop around Slade's plan. He didn't know if Kansas Jack would recognize him or not, but that was one chance the young half-breed could not afford to take, not if he wanted Wiley Bledsoe's killer. He had to light a shuck out of there, and fast.

Casually, he rose and strolled back into the bunkhouse. After dark, he would slip away. He was not worried so much over a confrontation as he was over the rustlers altering their plans about New Gideon. Chances were, when they discovered his disappearance, they would assume he had decided to drift. But he had to make sure that's exactly what Daughtery would think.

Inside the bunkhouse, he sprawled on his bunk and muttered to Rearden, "How long you figure it'll be before we move out?"

The boy shook his head. "Beats me."

He blew through his lips. "Sittin' around makes me restless. I like to be on the move."

"I reckon Mr. Daughtery will let us know when it's time."

"Hope it's soon. Else, I might just pull up stakes and hit the grubline. Maybe head up to Fort Dodge."

Joe Rearden didn't want to see Slade leave. He replied hurriedly, "I bet it won't be long. Probably a couple days."

127

Slade nodded. He had planted the seed in the boy's mind. Next morning when Slade turned up missing, Joe Rearden would tell of this conversation.

The young half-breed lay in the dark listening as the last man dropped into a deep slumber. The bunkhouse echoed with snores. He waited until early morning when sleep was deepest. Silently, Slade crawled from his soogan, rolled it up, and slipped out the door.

The main house slept silently.

The barn sprawled dark and ominous in the starlight. Slade ran in a crouch across the bare yard to the barn where he paused in its shadows to listen for any out-of-the-ordinary sounds before opening the door. To the south, a great bank of dark clouds filled with orange lightning and distant thunder rolled toward the ranch. He glanced at the great bear, his eyes instinctively focusing on the three stars in the tail. Sunrise in a couple hours. About the time the storm would hit. Slade grinned inwardly. If he could reach the storm, he was safe. Once again, he searched around him.

Satisfied that he had disturbed no one, Slade opened the door and froze.

The starlight glistened off the barrels of the revolvers that John Daughtery and

Kansas Jack held trained on Slade. "Going somewhere, Slade?" The rustler boss drawled.

His mind raced. He might as well carry his bluff to the hilt. "Yep. Been getting restless. Just this evening, I told Joe that I might be pulling out."

"Is that a fact?" asked Daughtery with a sneer.

"Ask him if you don't believe me." He made a move to step around the two men, but Daughtery cocked his revolver.

"That's far enough. You just back up and head over to the ranch house, you hear?" Daughtery gestured to the house with the gun barrel.

Feigning anger, Slade snapped. "What the hell's wrong with you, Daughtery?"

His own tone sharp with suppressed anger, the rustler growled. "Just do what I say, or I'll blow a hole in you right here."

Slade shrugged. With a chuckle he replied, "Well, now, that's not an idea that I particularly care for."

"Then do what I say."

To the south, the growl of thunder rolled across the prairie. Jack went ahead and lit a lamp. Slade stepped into the parlor, squinting his eyes against the sudden glare of lamplight. He carried his soogan under his left arm. His right arm hung loosely by his side, his hand only inches from his revolver.

As he turned to face the two men, he flipped the rawhide loop from the hammer of his revolver during that brief moment when his body shielded the move. "Now, just what in the hell is going on, Daughtery?" He tried to inject just the right degree of impatience in his voice, at the same time wondering where Kansas Jack's sidekick was.

Daughtery nodded to Kansas Jack. "Jack here says he run across you and some old man with an Injun out on the Staked Plains."

Jack nodded emphatically. "Damned 'pache, that's what he were."

The young half-breed studied Jack through narrowed eyes. "Lot of people look like me," he replied with a sarcastic drawl.

Jack's eyes gleamed like a rogue wolf's. "Maybe, maybe, but not ever' jasper totes a war club on his belt," he sneered, pointing the muzzle of his revolver to the club on Slade's hip.

Slade shrugged at Daughtery. "I recollect some saddle tramp stopping in for a handout with me and a jasper I met on the trail. Wasn't no redstick around though, just me and an old boy from Santa Fe who was heading to Fort Worth." He turned his eyes on Kansas Jack. "Yep, somebody stopped by. It might have been this one. I don't know. I don't keep up with trash." Kansas Jack stiffened and took a step forward. Daughtery stopped him and said, "I'm where I am today, Mr. Slade, because I never take chances. I've got a little bell in my head that rings when something seems out of kilter. Right now, that bell is ringing like a church bell celebrating Christmas."

A small grin tugged at Slade's thin lips. He decided to see how far he could push Kansas Jack. Maybe far enough to back him off his claim. Imperceptibly, he moved his hand closer to his revolver. "I don't know so much about the bells, but I do know that I don't answer to saddle tramps like this one."

"Why you —"

"Hold it, Jack," Daughtery said quickly.

Jack turned baleful eyes on John Daughtery. "He's callin' me a liar. Nobody ever called me that an' lived to brag about it." The outlaw trembled in rage.

Daughtery's face darkened. "I'm telling you to calm down. I'm handling this."

Slade threw some coal oil on the fire his words had stirred up in Kansas Jack. "What happened to all them that called you a liar,

Jack? You shoot 'em in the back?"

Kansas Jack exploded. He whirled and drew his revolver. At the same time, Daughtery cursed and slammed his own revolver across Jack's forearm. Jack screamed and his gun clattered to the floor.

Before Daughtery could recover, Slade threw his soogan at both of the men and pulled his own .44. "That's it, Daughtery. Hold it right there."

The tall man froze, his face hard beneath his white beard. His black eyes burned with hatred.

Slade stayed in his role as an owlhoot. "I told you, Mr. Daughtery. I'm a restless man. I don't cotton to sitting around, doing nothing. I got a Texas Ranger on my trail, and the longer I sit in one spot, the closer he gets." He motioned to the door. "Now, you and Jack are going to keep me company out to the barn."

"Think again, mister." The voice from behind froze Slade, but he kept his .44 on Daughtery and Jack.

Jack's red-rimmed eyes glowered with satisfaction.

"Just drop the gun," the voice said.

Slade struggled to pick up the voice's location. It was behind him, but he was unable to pinpoint just where. Jack took a step forward, but stopped when Slade turned the muzzle toward him.

The voice spoke again, this time from a different spot. "I ain't tellin' you no more, mister. Drop the gun." The sharp click of a cocking hammer cut the stillness of the parlor.

Reluctantly, Slade lowered his revolver.

In one quick motion, Kansas Jack stepped forward and swung a roundhouse right at Slade. The young half-breed ducked under the charging man's swing, slammed a hard fist into Jack's kidney, and spun him around to use him as a shield. Suddenly, everything went black.

CHAPTER TWELVE

John Daughtery stood over the inert body of Jake Slade. He holstered the revolver he had used to coldcock the young half-breed. "Tie him tight," he ordered Jack and the third man. "Then go get that Rearden kid."

While the third man brought Rearden, Jack dragged Slade into another room. The outlaw returned just as a sleepy-eyed Joe Rearden stumbled in, pulling his suspenders over his long johns. "You wanted to see me, Mr. Daughtery?" Joe dug his knuckles into his eyes.

"Yeah, Joe-Boy. Jack here was interested in that story of yours, the one about how you and Slade come to meet up in the cottonwood grove back southeast of here."

Rearden's young face blanched. He gulped, his Adam's apple a thick knot in his throat and bobbing like a cork. "Y-yessir."

"Tell Jack what happened. I forgot some of the details."

Joe Rearden shrugged and ducked his head. "It was nothin', Mr. Daughtery, especially nothin' to talk about."

Jack insisted. "I'd like to hear it."

The young boy looked up at John Daughtery, wide-eyed like a hog-tied calf. His cheeks burned red. His bottom lip quivered. "I-I lied to you, Mr. Daughtery. I didn't kill that redstick like I said." He hesitated, drew a deep breath, and continued. "It was Slade. He shot and killed that red devil just before I got my belly opened up." His words tumbled out as he cleansed his conscience of one of the only lies he had ever fabricated. "I didn't want you to think light of me, so I asked Slade to say I done it." For a moment, Joe Rearden looked at the two men briefly, then dropped his eyes.

John Daughtery stepped forward and rested a fatherly hand on the boy's shoulder. "That's okay, Joe. I understand. Don't be ashamed. It took a big man to admit the truth."

Joe looked up gratefully. "Thanks, Mr. Daughtery." He cut his eyes toward Kansas Jack sheepishly.

"Go on back to the bunk house, Joe-Boy. We're pulling out in an hour or so. Don't forget your rain gear. We're in for some weather."

Daughtery turned to Jack after Joe left. "I suspected something like that. Joe-Boy couldn't stomp on a spider, less kill an Injun."

Jack frowned. "I don't follow you."

Daughtery contained his disgust at Jack's lack of perception. The outlaw was dull and unimaginative, but, Daughtery reminded himself, that was the kind of man he had to work with. "Let me put it so you can understand, Jack. I'll give you ten to one odds that you won't find a dead Indian out in that cottonwood grove."

The outlaw's frown deepened. "Why not? Wolves drag the body away?"

Frustration swept over the tall rustler. Wearily, he shook his head. "No, Jack. There's no body there because Slade didn't kill the Indian." Without waiting for Jack's next question, Daughtery continued. "That was the same Indian you saw with Slade on the trail. For whatever reason, Slade wanted in with us, and he saw Joe-Boy as the belled steer." He paused, then added, "We were set up at Fort Sherman. Slade was the only one new to the organization. No way I could figure anyone else getting word to the army — probably through the Injun."

Jack nodded slowly, understanding seeping into his dull brain like water attempting to penetrate clay. Daughtery continued, forgetting about Kansas Jack as his own thoughts leaped forward in spontaneous conjecture. "He had to have been aware of our presence in order to plan such an elaborate scheme. That means he is either a lawman who is setting us up for a trap, or he's what he wants us to believe, a drifter who stumbled onto a grubline that served nothing but steak."

Daughtery shook his head as he remembered Slade's daring and cool thinking back at Fort Sherman. No, he told himself. He's no drifter. Drifters have no sense of direction, no goals. Slade was one of the most purposeful men Daughtery had ever met. On the other hand, the young half-breed did not have the smell of a lawman about him either.

"So, what do we do with him?" Kansas Jack reached for his revolver.

"We wait, dammit. We ride out in an hour for New Gideon. I don't have time to question him like I want, so he stays here under guard until I get back."

Disappointed, Jack holstered his gun.

With Daughtery in the lead, the rustlers rode out to the southeast just as the storm struck. Rain fell in sheets, whipped across the prairie by gale force winds. Daughtery left two men to watch Slade with instructions to keep the half-breed bound except for grub and toilet.

Faint voices penetrated the blackness surrounding Slade. Slowly the darkness faded into light behind his closed lids. He tried to open his eyes, but his muscles refused to function. Voices slowly penetrated his stupor.

"What you think Daughtery, he will do with this hombre?" A voice spoke in a distinct Hispanic accent.

"Who cares? I'd just as soon put a lead plumb between his eyes and tell Daughtery that God done took him."

"No. Mr. Daughtery, he say he want nothing to happen to this one."

Outside, thunder boomed, and the rain clattered into the window like hail on a tin roof. Slade drifted somewhere between consciousness and unconsciousness until the words of one of his guards sliced through the torpor engulfing him.

The second voice continued. "Who's that Bledsoe feller the boys was chewing over before they rode out, Segura?"

Bledsoe! Slade forced himself to listen.

Segura replied. "That is how Daughtery, he learns what is — ah — *acontecer* — what you would say, is happening down in the village of Mormons." The Mexican paused, then added with a touch of smugness. "Daughtery must feel a great loss with his man in the village dead."

"What happened to him?"

"I do not know. I hear he was dead. From what I hear, he *matado,* killed by a senorita."

Slade was fully awake now. Something nagged at him, something he should remember. He pushed the worry aside as the men continued their conversation.

"A female? I didn't know Daughtery had a woman on his payroll."

"He pay no senorita."

"Then where'd she come from? How'd she do Bledsoe in?"

"*¿Quién sabe? * Who knows? What I hear is *el rumor,* just talk. I think that is all it is, talk." He paused, then added lewdly, "Maybe the senorita was his *la puta,* his whore, or maybe the one they say who gave him gold."

Despite the excitement caused by the new information, Slade lay motionless for another ten minutes before feigning awakening. Outside, the sun had risen, but the storm continued, painting the day dark as dusk.

Slade groaned and tried to sit up against a

wall, but his bonds were too tight. He looked up into the sneering faces staring down at him. "Don't reckon I can get a lick of water, can I?"

The first man's sneer broadened. "I had my way, you'd have no need for water."

Segura said, "Remember Daughtery's orders."

The first man nodded in disgust and reached for a canteen while Segura helped Slade sit up against the wall. He held the canteen to Slade's lips. Slade drank copiously. When he finished, he nodded. "Obliged." He leaned back and closed his eyes, but his brain raced with the possibilities of what had taken place while he had been unconscious.

The two owlhoots went back to their poker game.

The clock on the mantel tolled ten. Slade guessed that the rustlers had probably left around sunrise, maybe before. That meant they had a four-to-six hour lead. He studied the room. On one end of the table on which the two men played cards lay Slade's weapons, his .44, the war club, knife, and his slingshot. He glanced out the window at the driving rain.

"When do you leave to meet Daughtery?"

Segura glanced at the clock. "Midnight.

The ride, it is many hours to the river."

Slade glanced around the room. Where was Nana? Surely he would have noticed that Slade had not ridden out with the rustlers. Had they caught him? No. There was no white man alive who could trap Nana.

Not long afterward, a face appeared in the rain-distorted window behind the two men. Slade grinned. Nana. Moments later, the back door slammed open in the kitchen, and the wind drove the rain inside.

The two men raced from the room, their handguns drawn.

Slade heard two grunts, then Nana appeared in the doorway, a broad grin on his face.

"What kept you?" Slade rolled over so Nana could slash his bonds.

"I thought you rode with the rustlers. When I see someone rides the roan, I come back."

Slade rose quickly and gathered his weapons.

Throwing his saddle on a short-coupled sorrel, Slade said, "I figure they'll hole up after noon. They'll rest their animals until dark. My guess is they'll hit New Gideon whenever the storm breaks."

"You are certain that is where they go?"

Slade glanced across his saddle at Nana. "Yes."

Without another word, the two men mounted and headed southeast. The rain had washed out all sign, but Slade knew that John Daughtery and his band were ahead. The trick now was to reach New Gideon first.

CHAPTER THIRTEEN

The storm continued unabated throughout the day. Slade had seen gully washers like this before, but usually down on the Gulf coast. He did remember an old timer at Adobe Walls swearing that those Gulf storms sometimes could reach this far north into the state. Maybe that was the explanation.

The only consolation Slade could find in the storm was that Daughtery was facing it also. The violent weather had to hamper the rustlers just as it did Slade and Nana.

Just before dusk, the rain slackened; the clouds parted, providing starlight by which they could travel. From time to time, clouds heavy with rain moved over, dropping another deluge, halting their travel. Just as Slade and Nana topped the rim of the valley overlooking New Gideon, another downpour struck, forcing them into the scanty protection of a small motte of stunted oak. When the clouds finally parted, leaving clear skies filled with freshly washed stars, the young half-breed glanced at the great bear in the northern skies. Almost one o'clock. They had been holed up by the last storm for almost three hours.

Peering down into the valley lit by a waxing moon rising over the eastern rim of the sprawling basin, Slade grinned. The village was dark. He had half expected to see the small town ablaze with lights. The darkness could mean that he had reached town ahead of Daughtery. With a click of his tongue, Slade urged the sorrel down into the valley.

Fifteen minutes later, Slade, with Nana at his side, knocked on Joseph Ware's door.

Across the street, Aaron Smith, returning from his brother's home, paused beneath an elm as the blacksmith opened the door for the two men. He scowled and stepped behind the broad bole of the tree. After the door closed, the Stake counselor slipped into the shadows along the buildings and made his way home.

Inside, Slade and Nana faced Joseph Ware and Three-Fingers Bent across the kitchen table. The regulator clock on the mantel struck midnight. The broad-shouldered blacksmith stared at the two men incredulously as Slade related the events of the last several days including the intended raid tonight. Mrs. Ware peered from around the doorjamb, but when Slade told of Bledsoe's involvement, she came to stand beside her husband, her own shyness outweighed by Slade's stunning allegations.

Ware shook his large head. "But you got no proof."

"Not yet, but I'll have it when we catch Daughtery and his men. I've never seen one owlhoot who'd swing for another. They'll be so anxious to spill what they know that you'll have to beat 'em off with a stick."

"I'll round up some men," Ware said.

Slade nodded and said to Nana. "I reckon you'd better light a shuck out of here. Just keep us in sight."

Nana grunted and headed for the door, but Ware stopped him. "No. He comes with us."

The young half-breed grinned wryly. "That's not smart. Some of your people don't care much for Indians, especially Apache."

Ware colored. "Maybe not, but if he leaves, and something goes wrong out there, then that'll be proof enough to some people around here that you and Bent are in cahoots with the rustlers."

Slade glanced at Bent who nodded agreement with Ware. Nana's expression remained impassive. He didn't like the idea, but it did make sense. "All right," said Slade.

Within ten minutes, Ware had rounded up two dozen men, many of whom were accompanied by their wives and curious neighbors, for in any frontier village, any kind of meeting, day or night, drew a crowd. They met Slade in the stable behind Ware's house. Each eyed Nana warily, but no word was spoken. Even Garth Smith remained silent.

"Here they are, Slade," said Ware, gesturing to the gathering crowd.

Slade quickly told them the same story he had earlier related to Ware. "From what Joseph says, your herd's nighting back east downriver."

"A couple miles," volunteered a young man with freckles.

Ware arched an eyebrow. "I thought you was riding herd tonight, Tom."

The young man grinned. "The nighthawk relieved me about an hour ago."

Ware glanced at Slade. "This here's Tom Duggan."

Slade nodded, unable to believe his good luck in beating Daughtery to the herd. He looked at the circle of faces around him. "Has anybody seen or heard anything out of the ordinary in the last few hours?"

Constance Young held up her hand timidly.

Ware recognized her. "What is it, Miss Young?"

Shyly, she looked around. "It might be nothing, Brother Ware, but about two hours ago, I looked out my window and saw some riders heading south."

"Indians?"

"White men. I could make them out in the starlight."

Excited, Ware looked around at Slade. "Do we follow 'em?"

Puzzled now as to Daughtery's destination, Slade considered Ware's question. Something nagged at him, but he could not pinpoint just what it was. "No. If that was them, we'd better get to the herd fast in case they swing around on us."

Twenty minutes later, the band of men discovered the two nighthawks sprawled in the mud, both dead. The herd was missing.

Nana and Slade spoke softly, and the Apache disappeared into the night.

"Where's the Injun going?" Garth Smith growled.

Slade looked at the young boy. "Same place all of us are, looking for sign. It can't be more than an hour old. Two hundred head leaves a wide track. Now, all of you, spread out and see what you can find. Meet back here in about a half hour."

"Bent goes with me," Garth Smith insisted. He glanced at Ware. "This could be a trick."

Slade reined his sorrel around, but Bent stopped him. "It ain't worth the argue, Jake. I'll go with the kid."

The young half-breed nodded. "Joseph and me will head south, see if we can cut the sign of those other riders."

Thirty minutes later, the group reassembled in a grove of cottonwoods. Nana was the last to arrive. He shook his head. Slade frowned. "It doesn't make sense."

"What don't?" Ware frowned.

Slade gestured to the weather. "No sign. Despite the rain, there would have been something, especially on the rim. The runoff would wash away tracks on the side of the valley, but up on the rim where the prairie is flat, there should have been some sign —" He paused, then glanced around the circle of faces. "If," he added. "If it has been only an hour."

"What do you mean by that?" demanded Garth Smith.

Ignoring the question, Slade stared at the young man with freckles. "You sure you was relieved an hour ago, Tom?"

The young man coughed. "Well, it's been more than an hour now." His voice was nervous.

Slade knew then that the young man was lying. "The ground's soggy with mud, but there's no way that much sign could melt away in an hour. It'd take at least three or four hours."

As one, the other men turned to stare at the young man. Ware spoke for all of them. "The truth, Tom. The truth."

For a moment, the young man stared defiantly at Joseph Ware, but his resolve quickly faded. He ducked his head. "I paid Billy to take my shift tonight," he said lamely.

Nana grunted. Slade nodded at his Apache brother. "I'd guess at least four hours. Not much longer." He turned to Ware. "If we ride hard, we might be able to intercept them at the North Canadian."

"What about our dead?"

Slade saw the pain in Aaron Smith's eyes. He nodded to the freckle-faced young man who had lied to them. "Put 'em on his horse. Let him walk 'em back."

As soon as the dead boys were lashed to the horse, Slade led the remaining men to the northwest, telling them of Daughtery's ranch. "If we get ahead of them, we can jump them when they cross the North Canadian."

Garth Smith rode up beside him. "How do you know where they'll cross?"

He shrugged. "I don't, but if I was in his shoes, there's two natural crossings that I would consider pushing a herd through. We'll put men out at each one. Your father can take one, and I'll take the other." Slade directed his next words to the craggy-faced man. "As soon as you spot the herd, put a man on your fastest horse and send him for us. We'll do the same should we spot them."

"What if we miss them? What if they take the herd across somewhere else?" asked Ware.

"Then we'll have to do some tracking."

Aaron Smith shook his head. "I don't like the idea of us being separated. I think we should stay together."

"I don't like it either, but we got enough guns that we should be able to stand them off until reinforcements reach us."

Smith stared at Slade several long seconds before giving in. "All right, but I still don't like it."

Later, eight miles to the north, John Daughtery reined up at the base of a sandstone bluff. Kansas Jack pulled up beside him.

"Why are we stopping? If we keep pushing, we'll get across the river before sunrise."

The lanky rancher shook his head. A chill ran down his spine as he stared at the dark caves in the bluff. He had expected a cheery fire. Instead, only a darkness greeted him. "Something's wrong. Segura was supposed to meet us here."

Ed Towers rode up. "What's wrong?"

Daughtery nodded to the sandstone bluff before them. "Segura's not here."

Towers grunted. "The greaser probably got hisself drunk." The hulking foreman's words were a sneer.

Daughtery didn't buy Towers' explanation. "Not José. He's always been reliable, even if he is a greaser. More so than most white men." He shook his head. "No. Something — or someone — stopped him."

"Slade?"

Daughtery turned the idea over in his mind. "Could be." He peered into the darkness to the west. If Slade had managed to escape, he would be coming from the west. "Take the herd north, Ed. We're not taking any chances."

Towers nodded.

Slade dropped the men off along the North Canadian with a reminder to send a rider as soon as the herd was sighted. By the time the second group was positioned, a pale sun struggled to burn through the wet haze that enveloped the river.

Remembering Joe's talk about Daughtery's ranch north of New Gideon, Slade, Nana, and Joseph Ware rode east along the river to the shallow water crossing that lay due north of the Mormon village.

The fog had thinned somewhat by midmorning as the trio rounded a bend in the river. Nana, in the lead, reined up abruptly, so abruptly that Ware's horse crowhopped.

"What is it?" Slade squinted into the fog.

Even before Nana answered, Slade saw the churned up riverbank ahead. "Damn," he muttered, spurring his sorrel forward to the crossing.

"What's wrong?" Ware frowned.

Ignoring the question, the two men studied the sign with keen eyes.

"About sunrise, I guess." Slade looked at Nana. "They moved faster than I figured."

The Apache grunted his assent.

The half-breed pulled his .44 and spun the cylinder. "We ride hard, we catch them."

By now, Joseph Ware had figured out what was going on. The audacity of Slade's unspoken plan appalled him. "Hold on. The three of us are no match for them. We need reinforcements."

Slade studied Ware a moment. The black-smith was right. But maybe Slade and Nana could hold the rustlers at bay until help arrived. If nothing else, at least they could track Daughtery, then strike when the others arrived. He nodded. "Get the others, Joseph, then cut across country to intersect the trail. We'll leave sign."

Ware started to protest, but from the firm expression on Slade's face, he knew any dissent would be of no avail. He nodded and slammed his heels into his horse.

"And hurry," yelled Slade after the disappearing man.

Two hours later, Slade and Nana spotted the herd on the horizon, a thin, dark line between the greenish gray prairie and the blue sky. The Apache arched an eyebrow. His dark eyes flashed as he studied the vast prairie surrounding them. "Kiowa country," he said.

Slade flung an impatient glance over his shoulder even though he knew it was much too soon to expect Ware and the others. Nana grinned at the impatience on his brother's face. "Do not expect the others until after the sun is overhead."

A rueful grin split Slade's dark face. "You always know best, don't you?"

Nana's grin broadened. "Apaches are the true human beings. That is why we know best. Listen to what I say, my brother." He slid off his mustang and whipped the blanket from the animal's back. "The herd goes nowhere that we cannot follow." He spread his blanket on the ground in the shade of his horse and sat on his heels.

Slade glanced at the dark line that was the herd. Nana was right. The herd was going nowhere they could not follow. At the most, the rustlers would make five or six miles before the reinforcements arrived. A rare chuckle escaped Slade's lips. He dismounted and loosened the cinch.

He squatted in the shade of his sorrel and chewed some jerky and drank from his canteen. Dragging the back of his hand across his lips, he lay back on the wiry prairie grass and closed his eyes.

Moments later, Nana grunted with satisfaction as Slade's breathing became regular and deep. The Apache brave lay back himself and quickly fell asleep.

When Slade awakened, the sun was directly overhead, but Nana had rigged a canvas fly that cast a small patch of shade over the two of them. Sitting up and stretching, Slade grunted at his Apache brother. "What time is it?"

"Time for the others to be here."

Slade sensed a faint touch of impatience in Nana's voice. He rose and looked over their back trail. Heat rose in waves, contorting the distant prairie like cut glass. Quickly he considered their options. "We'll leave sign," he said abruptly, turning to the sorrel and tightening the cinch. "Maybe they'll catch up with us before we reach the herd."

He swung onto the sorrel and hesitated. Far to the south, two dots appeared on the horizon.

"Ware and another one," announced Nana.

Slade didn't dispute Nana's word. As a boy, the Apache brave had exhibited keen eyesight, eyesight that Slade learned to trust.

They rode to meet the two men.

The riders were Ware and the freckle-faced young man who had lied.

Ignoring the young man, Slade looked at Ware. "What's he doing here? Where are the others?"

"Gone. Back to New Gideon. Took Bent with them." He gestured to the young man by his side. "Tom here took the two boys back to town and then hustled back out here to help. He was the only one I could talk into coming on up here with me."

"It was Garth Smith that twisted their

thinkin'," said the young man. "He talked the others into believing that you were leading them through the briar patch."

A wave of anger swept over Slade, then dissipated quickly. "What about you?" He eyed the young man's sweaty horse. "Why did you come back?"

"Because," the young man replied, his face pale, but his jaw set. "I was responsible. I couldn't not come back."

Slade studied the younger man. He might be young and inexperienced, but Slade admired his determination. "This show isn't going to be like wrangling a few head of beef. There's nine of them and only four of us. And these yahoos shoot to kill."

"Maybe so, but if I hadn't offered Billy money to take my place, he'd be alive now."

"But you'd be dead."

The younger man looked into Slade's face. His eyes reflected his anguish. "I reckon that's just about how I feel."

Slade glanced at Ware, who shrugged his shoulders. He looked back to the freckle-faced man. "Okay, Tom. Let's ride."

They caught up with Daughtery two hours later as the rustlers drove the herd onto the high plains. Slade pulled into a shallow arroyo and turned to the others. "Daughtery has a ranch somewhere north of here. They're not pushing the herd, so they must not figure on any pursuit. Nana and me'll work ahead." He nodded to Ware. "You two tag after the herd. When you hear us open up on 'em, you hit 'em from the rear."

Ware removed his hat and wiped his face with a red bandanna. "You been in this part of the country before?"

"Not north of the Canadian."

"Then let me go with you. Your friend here can stay behind with Tom. I've been through here a few times. I know where we can wait for 'em."

Slade studied the older man. He nodded. "How far?"

"Five or six miles. The trail crosses a river and then narrows into a pass between two bluffs on the far side of the river."

"What about cover?"

"Not much. Some sage on the prairie, but we can hide amongst the boulders on the cliffs."

In his mind's eye, Slade pictured the bluffs and the river. "How wide is this river?"

"Narrow. Couple hundred feet."

"How do we get ahead of them?"

Ware pointed to the west. "There's enough cover to the west to hide us. We make a big circle and come in from the north."

Slade turned to Nana. "Stay as close to the herd as you can without letting them see you. When you hear us fire, rush 'em from the rear." He paused. "But watch out for the herd. Those cows'll stampede like hell."

Nana nodded his agreement and glanced at Tom. The young man's jaw twitched nervously. His Adam's apple bobbed.

Slade and Ware circled west of the trail and came in from the north. From a distance, the blacksmith pointed out the bluffs on either side of the pass. Slade studied the lay of the land from their concealment in a narrow wash.

Across the river, the slowly moving line of beeves trudged down off the prairie onto the river flats, which extended a mile to the south of the river.

Ware whispered, "Looks like we made it in time."

"Wait 'til we're there before you brag too much," Slade replied, his tone cautious.

Ware led the way down the wash, which skirted the sandstone bluffs. Slade followed, nervously glancing at the cliffs above the pass, a natural spot for an ambush. And if he recognized it as such, he was certain its value had not been lost on John Daughtery.

The narrow wash opened into a coulee choked with cedar. The coulee twisted in a serpentine fashion behind the bluffs, perhaps, Slade hoped, providing a likely trail to a spot above the pass.

As they made their way up through the coulee, Slade kept glancing at the bluffs rising above them. At a cedar thicket on the rim of the coulee, Slade hissed at Ware. "Hold up."

"What's wrong?"

Slade pulled up beside the blacksmith and pointed through the stunted growth of cedar rising over their heads, hiding them from searching eyes on the bluffs above. "I don't know. A hunch. If I've ever seen a spot for an ambush, this is it."

Ware beamed. "I told you so."

"For them, too," Slade said.

A frown erased the grin on Ware's face as Slade's implication became clear. "You mean — Daughtery? Would he take that kind of precaution?"

"John Daughtery might be a rustler, but that doesn't mean he's dead from the neck up. He's smart. My guess is that he's smart enough to hedge his bet by sending someone ahead to make sure everything's clear." Slade dismounted and handed his reins to Ware. "I figure they're watching the trail on the far side of the bluff, but you never can tell. Someone might be perched up there watching this side, too. Wait here until I see what's up there."

Dropping into a crouch, the young half-breed slipped along the coulee, his moccasined feet light as a black widow's over a taut web. He crawled out of the coulee and hid beneath a scrubby cedar by the edge of the trail. Less than fifty yards away, the road narrowed between two perpendicular cliffs, at the top of which stretched sandstone ledges littered with boulders the size of houses.

Slade studied the sagebrush-covered slope leading to the ledges for any spot large enough to conceal a man. He saw nothing. He studied the ledges. Still nothing. Heaving a sigh of relief, he rose and started to call Ware up when he froze.

CHAPTER FOURTEEN

A half-smoked cigarette came spinning over the ledge, trailing a looping string of smoke in the still air. Slade dropped to his stomach behind the cedar.

His intuition had been right once again. As a boy, he had been taught to rely on his hunches. At first, he experienced much difficulty interpreting uncertain instincts, and when he did, Slade was distrustful of their demands, but under the patient guidance of Gokhlayeh, the young half-breed came to understand the relationship between knowledge and intuition.

Now he watched the ledge, his ears tuned for human sound. The metallic clink of a spur broke the stillness. He waited. No further sounds followed, but the single, faint rustle of metal had been enough for Slade's keen ears to place the location of the man on the ledge.

More silently than the mountain rattler,

Slade slithered through the underbrush to the rim of the ledge. Removing his slouch hat, he peered through the sage. The guard sat on a boulder. Slade glanced at the ledge on the far side of the pass. He saw no one among the boulders. A frown knitted his brows. If he had been in Daughtery's place, he would have stationed a guard on either ledge. The rustler leader's seeming lack of detail bothered Slade.

Turning his attention back to the guard, Slade retrieved his slingshot from his vest pocket and glanced around for a proper stone, but there were none among the litter of sandstone talus. Rounded stones flew truer than those with flat sides, which flared to one side or the other. He settled for one shaped like a pecan.

He looked back at the guard. The distance was not far, perhaps thirty feet, maybe forty. He then studied the oblong stone in his hand. At such a short distance, it would not flare too wide.

Once again Slade glanced at the ledge on the far side of the pass, then he rose to his feet and whipped the slingshot over his head. The rawhide strings hummed like bees.

The sound carried through the still air. The guard stiffened. Just as he started to look around, Slade released the rock. At the last moment, the projectile flared slightly, catching the guard a glancing blow on his forehead instead of the temple where Slade had aimed.

The blow was enough to stagger the guard, causing him to drop his Winchester with a clatter to the stone ledge. Faster than a striking snake, Slade raced across the clearing and finished the job with the muzzle of his revolver.

Just as he turned to call Ware up, a rifle roared, and a slug tore his slouch hat from his head. Slade dropped behind a boulder. Another shot rang out from the ledge across the pass. A slug slammed into the sandstone wall behind him, peppering his back with grains of sand and shards of lead.

Slade cursed himself for moving too fast. If he had been patient, if he had waited before jumping the first guard, he might have spotted the second one. He peered around the boulder.

A third shot rang out, followed by wild yells and gunfire from below. A rumble like thunder shook the ground. Stampede! He grinned. Nana and Tom were doing their job.

Another slug slammed into the wall behind him. Jumping to his feet, Slade threw four quick shots at the boulder behind which the rifleman was hiding. In the same motion, he raced for the rim of the ledge and slid behind a patch of sage.

From this vantage point, he searched for the stampeding herd, expecting to see the lead animals hitting the river. Another shot rang out behind him. The rifleman fired at Slade's original position, not having seen him sprint across the ledge.

Slade froze when he saw the herd. The animals were stampeding away from the river, back on Nana and Tom Duggan. At the rear of the herd rode Daughtery and his men, shouting wildly and firing their revolvers into the air.

All Slade could do was watch helplessly as the herd lumbered across the flats and disappeared onto the prairie. Slade realized then that the firing behind him had stopped.

The clatter of hoofbeats sounded on the road below. Suddenly a rider shot into sight, his heels spurring his animal, and his free hand grasping his saddle gun. Slade raised his .44, then lowered it. Facing a man was one thing. Backshooting was another.

Ignoring the unconscious guard, Slade raced back to the coulee where Joseph waited. The thundering of the herd was growing distant by the time the two men crossed the shallow river and took up pursuit of the stampeding beeves.

Faint gunfire reached Slade's ears. Nana and Tom, he guessed. A splattering of gunfire responded, then silence. Slade grimaced. He knew what had happened.

Nana and Duggan, anticipating the stampede to be heading in the opposite direction, must have been caught by surprise. Slade was not worried about his Apache brother, but the young boy, Tom Duggan, was another matter.

A cry caught Slade's attention. In the distance where the river flats climbed onto the prairie, Nana stood on top of a drift of debris, logs and limbs and trash deposited by the last flood. Slade yelled at Ware and pointed to the Apache.

Nana knelt beside Tom Duggan, who lay behind a giant log. "The boy. He is bad."

Quickly Slade gently unbuttoned the youth's bloody shirt. A slug was lodged in the boy's chest.

Ware looked down from his horse. "Bad?" When Slade failed to answer, Ware continued, "Can you fix him up?"

Slade shook his head. "We need to get him back to town, to a real doctor. The slug's close to his heart."

165

Ware grimaced. "But the rustlers —"

"Don't worry. We spooked them away from here. The only place they can go now is Daughtery's other ranch back west." He nodded at the pale-faced boy gasping for breath. "We need to get this button back home. Nana will trail Daughtery."

Nana looked at Slade and nodded. He knew what his brother expected of him.

Quickly building a travois from debris found along the riverbank, Slade and Ware headed for New Gideon, pausing only to give the wounded man water and repack his wound against fresh bleeding. They rode through the night, reaching New Gideon just before sunrise.

A crowd gathered quickly as Ware and Slade carried the wounded man inside the doctor's house. When they came out of the house, the crowd had doubled. Questions were hurled at the two men. Ware held up his hand for silence. When the crowd grew quiet, he briefly sketched out the events of the last few days.

Then he added, "Slade here knows where the rustlers are taking the cattle. If enough of us get together, we can go up there and take them back."

Garth Smith stepped forward, a sneer on

his face as he glared at Slade. "You didn't have much luck when you tried to ambush them. But then maybe you didn't try too hard."

Bent pushed through the crowd and stopped at Slade's side. "Maybe they mighta if you damned cowards hadn't hightailed it home soon as they rode out of sight."

Smith made a threatening step forward, but Bent held his ground, his eyes cold and his jaw set. The older man hissed. "Come on, sonny. You got the guts, you just come on."

Aaron Smith laid a restraining hand on his son's arm. The older man's voice thundered over the crowd. "First things first, Mr. Slade. What about Wiley Bledsoe's killer? You said you would find him."

The silence hanging over the crowd was filled with growing anticipation as Slade stared back at Aaron Smith. "That's right, Mr. Smith. I said I would."

"Well?"

The young half-breed glanced at Bent, then turned back to Aaron Smith. He did not want to reveal the slim leads he had. "The answer is with John Daughtery and his men. They talked about Bledsoe." Slade hesitated, deciding to say nothing of the woman.

Aaron Smith's eyes narrowed, and his thin lips curled in a mocking grin. "You're beating around the bush, Mr. Slade. Did you find out who killed Wiley Bledsoe?"

Smith had Slade nailed to the wall.

"Well?"

Slade shook his head. "All I can tell you is that one of the rustlers mentioned that Bledsoe worked for the rustlers. Once I get my hands on Daughtery, then I'll find the killer."

A loud guffaw sounded from the rear of the crowd. A voice cried out, "Stop crowhopping, Slade. The old man did it."

Several voices joined in agreement with the first.

"Hold on," barked Slade. "Look, you've given me this much time. Go with me after the rustlers. When we catch them, you'll discover the truth."

Joseph Ware spoke up. "I say we go with Slade. We've waited this long. If Bent is the killer, another few days won't change nothing. The judge will still be here."

A chorus of dissenting cries drowned Ware's words. When they died away, Ware spoke softly. "Do I have to remind you that we, of all people, should show understanding and compassion? After all, who here does not remember the terrible events that took place in 1858, just twelve short years ago, when our brethren massacred one hundred and forty innocent travelers, men, women, and children? Do we want another Mountain Meadows on our conscience?" He cut his blazing eyes to a hunchbacked older Saint nearby. "You remember it, Matthew Parchman. You were one of those the council sent to investigate the massacre."

Silence gripped the crowd with an icy hand. Before Matthew Parchman could reply, Garth Smith spoke up. "That kind of thing won't happen again"

"That's not the way I hear all of you talking now," Ware retorted.

An embarrassed silence fell over the men. A single voice from the rear said, "But if we go after them rustlers, some of us will be killed."

A muttering undertone spread through the crowd. Slade raised his voice above the noise. "Sure it's dangerous. I won't lie and tell you it isn't, but if you want your herd back, you're going to have to take 'em back — the same way they were taken from you."

By now the crowd numbered over a hundred. From the rear, a voice cried out, "We're not gunmen. We're farmers."

A muttering of consent greeted the man's words. Slade raised his arms for silence. "We don't need gunmen. We need those of you who aren't afraid to stand up and take back what's yours. But, that don't mean there won't be some fighting. Daughtery and his bunch won't turn the herd over to us like it was a birthday party. We *will* have to take it from them. And there *will* be some shooting, and maybe some killing."

His words were followed by an uncomfortable silence. Men ducked their heads, scuffed their toes in the dust.

Slade spoke again. "Maybe the day will come where we won't have to fight for what's ours. Sooner or later, that will be the way of this country. But now, here in New Gideon, you've got to stand tall and claim what is yours."

The door behind Slade opened. A frail voice spoke. "I'll go." Slade turned to see Tom Duggan, his chest wrapped in a blood-stained bandage, leaning against the doorjamb. Before Slade could reply, the freckle-faced young man collapsed.

Slade helped the doctor carry the young man back to his bed. Joseph Ware's angry voice came through the open door, shaming the men in the crowd. "I thought I knew you men. But I was wrong. Tom Duggan's got more guts in his little finger than all of you put together. You've fooled me, but you can't fool God, and if He's the God I've always believed Him to be, the One who had his Son run the money changers from the temple, then He's ashamed of you at this moment."

For several seconds after Joseph Ware finished, no one spoke. Finally Aaron Smith stepped up on the porch and turned to face the crowd. "Brother Ware is right. God helps those who help themselves. The Saints have always done for themselves. That is how we built this town. The only way we will have our herd returned is if we take it back ourselves. Although I disagree with Mr. Slade's reason for being here, and I still believe he is wrong about Mr. Bent, I, for one, will follow him. It is evident to me he does wish to help us. The least we can do is help ourselves. After all," he added, "have we already forgotten what we had to fight to get here?"

CHAPTER FIFTEEN

Just after sunrise, a party of twenty men rode out of New Gideon. Joseph Ware pulled up beside Slade. The wiry young half-breed glanced at the blacksmith. "You should have stayed behind and got some rest, Joseph."

Ware grunted. "That'll come. I'm sorry about Mr. Bent being kept behind. He wanted to come with us."

"Yep," said Slade. "But he understands. They think he's the killer, and they don't want to take a chance on losing him. The only problem," Slade added with a chuckle, "is that by the time I clear him, that old codger will have put on twenty pounds of your wife's fine cooking."

Ware patted his stomach and with a laugh, replied, "That's not hard to do, I guarantee you that." The blacksmith hesitated, then added, "And she'll enjoy his company." He laughed again. "Sometimes she fusses about

Constance Young dropping in so much or staying so long, but Mrs. Ware likes company even if she won't admit it. I don't know what I'd do without that woman."

Slade nodded. The blacksmith's words gave the young half-breed cause to reflect. He remembered the empty, frightened feeling that came over him when he finally understood that his own mother was dead, that never again would she be there to protect and comfort him.

Although he did have an Apache family, a void had remained in his life, one that was partially filled when he found his sister — fourteen years after she had been kidnapped. It was hard to believe so much time had passed.

That's where he should be now, back in Tucson waiting for her and her husband to arrive from California, not out here searching for a band of rustlers. He thought about his present situation, wondering just how in the hell it had become so twisted and tangled. Yet, he had learned during the War of Secession that those twists and tangles are a natural part of what the white man called *living*.

Not so the Indian. The Indian knew how to live, really live. He walked and played at Nature's side, going to the grave with no more than he brought into the world. Slade reckoned that no boy could have had a more satisfying childhood than that he had been given by the Apaches. A damned shame boys have to grow up, he told himself. And a damned shame the white man is trying to destroy the Indian's way of life.

The vast prairie of shortgrass and sage-brush spread around them like an ocean. The undulating sand hills on the horizon writhed and squirmed in the rising waves of heat. There are only two differences between late autumn and summer on the Texas prairie. The days are longer and the nights are hotter in the summer. The daytime heat is just as intense, the dust is just as choking, and the wind is just as searing.

There were no objections when Slade pulled up at the base of a sand hill at dusk. Small fires were quickly laid, horses un-saddled, and soogans unrolled. "Do you think the rustlers know we're following them?"

Slade nodded to the speaker. "They'd be fools if they didn't, and John Daughtery is no fool. But we'll know more later tonight."

Garth Smith looked up after dropping a johnnycake into grease sputtering in a fire-blackened spider, a three-legged skillet sitting on the edge of the coals. "What do you mean by that?"

Ware answered, "Slade's Apache brother, Nana."

"That's right. I'd forgotten all about him. Where is he?" Garth Smith glanced around suspiciously. "I haven't seen him lately."

Two or three men paused and looked up from their own chores. Slade spoke up. "I expect him in tonight. He's been following the rustlers since he left Joseph and me up north." The other men had moved in and were listening. Slade added, "So don't no one get spooked when he comes in."

"Are you sure you can trust him?"

Slade looked at the man who asked the question. "His folks took me in when I was eight. Nana and me have been brothers for sixteen years." He paused, and a droll smile curled his lips. "Yes. I can trust him."

His reply satisfied everyone, even Aaron and Garth Smith. They returned to their bedrolls and soon the rattling of snores filled the night.

As Slade and Ware sat around their fire, the cry of a whippoorwill cut through the chirruping of the crickets. Slade looked at Ware. "That's Nana."

Slade returned the call. Moments later, Nana slipped into camp without a sound. The three men huddled by the fire. Five minutes later, the Apache brave rose, nodded to Slade, and, like a puff of smoke, vanished into the night.

The next morning, Slade gathered the men. "We found out last night that Daughtery and his bunch pushed the herd past the North Canadian." He did not mention that Nana had also reported that at first Daughtery had pointed the herd to the southwest out of Indian Territory, crossed the North Canadian, and then for some reason, turned back north, and recrossed the river. He continued. "I sent Nana back to keep an eye peeled. He'll meet us at the river."

Just before noon, the men came upon Nana squatting by a small fire on the edge of a patch of shinnery a few miles south of the river. Half a dozen rabbits roasted on spits around the fire. The men needed no second invitation.

"The herd still moves west," the Apache said.

"How far?"

"Beyond the ranch one day."

"We can make that up easy enough," said Slade, pursing his lips at the information. Daughtery puzzled him. First, he headed southwest, then turned back, bypassing his own ranch.

Nana shrugged. "There are four waiting for you at the river."

"There's twenty of us. Let's just ride 'em down," said Garth Smith, his face flushed with excitement.

Shaking his head, Slade looked at Aaron Smith. "We do that, and some of us will go back draped over our saddles."

Aaron Smith cleared his throat. "Then, what do you suggest, Mr. Slade?"

"Give Nana and me time to slip behind them. Then you come riding up, but pull up just out of rifle range. They'll be too wrapped up with you to figure anyone is coming up on their backsides. If we're lucky, we can capture the four of them and maybe find out who really killed Wiley Bledsoe."

"I'll go with you," volunteered Joseph Ware. "There's four of them, so an extra hand might come in handy."

"We're going on foot," Slade warned. "The river's a few miles ahead, and we got to swing wide to stay out of their sight. It won't be no Sunday afternoon social."

Ware nodded his understanding. Slade was skeptical of the blacksmith's ability to make the run, but the burly man insisted. "Give us one hour, then head due north," Slade said to Aaron Smith. "When you near the river, you'll see a break in the cottonwood grove. Nana says it's a natural ford, and that's where Daughtery's men are waiting."

Smith nodded, his dark eyes losing some of their fierceness. "Good luck, Mr. Slade."

Slade stared into Smith's face for several seconds, seeing the sincerity in the older man's eyes. He nodded. "Thanks."

Nana led the way followed by Slade and Ware.

Joseph Ware dropped out after the first three miles. Slade and Nana continued, knowing Ware would make his way to the river once he caught his breath.

At the river, Slade and Nana rolled a drift log into the water and drifted downstream behind it, their rifles on top of the log to keep them dry. The Apache pointed out the positions of the four men as the log drifted past the crossing. Two were in trees, and two were behind rocks stacked into a makeshift breastwork.

One of the men in the trees pointed to the south. He had spotted the oncoming riders.

Slade frowned. The two behind the rocks were in front of the ones in the trees. That made the situation bad. Without emotion, Slade realized he and Nana could not take out those on the ground without being seen by the men in the trees, and there was no way to take out the men in the trees without a disturbance.

He pointed to one of the men in the trees. "He's yours. I got the other."

Nana did not reply.

In the distance, Aaron Smith halted the oncoming riders.

"Don't miss," whispered Slade, taking a bead on his man's thigh.

Neither missed.

With a scream of pain, both men tumbled from their perches in the trees. One landed on the back of his neck, snapping it and killing him instantly. The other landed on his back and lay still, knocked senseless.

The other two men leaped to their feet at the screams. Neither man was a quitter. When Slade called for them to throw down their guns, both men jerked their rifles to their shoulders and began firing.

Slade had no choice. He put two .44 slugs into one gunman's chest. Nana did the same to the other.

By the time the Mormons rode in, Slade had propped the wounded man against the trunk of a fallen cottonwood. Nana returned from the river, Slade's hat filled with water. At the half-breed's nod, the Apache threw the water in the rustler's face.

The man's bearded face twisted in agony

as his bony fingers dug into his thigh in an effort to alleviate the pain. Slade was puzzled. The man was a stranger. Had Daughtery picked up reinforcements?

The riders dismounted and gathered around the wounded rustler who glared up at the ring of accusing faces, his own blazing with belligerence. With a snarl, he said, "Dammit, don't just stand there gawking. Somebody put a patch on my leg."

His Winchester across his knee, Slade squatted in front of the man. "When the time comes."

The grizzled rustler stared at Slade, uncomprehending. Suddenly the belligerence fled his face, replaced with a frightened uncertainty.

Slade's lips were a thin, compressed line. He continued, "You got some answers for us. When I'm satisfied that you've told us the truth, you'll get some help. Now where's Daughtery taking the herd?"

The wounded man met Slade's eyes. "I ain't sayin' nothing. You'll —"

Slade dropped the butt of his carbine on the man's bleeding wound.

"Agggh — damn — don't — God, don't," the rustler screamed.

"Slade!" Aaron Smith took a tentative step forward but halted as Slade hissed over his

180

shoulder.

"Stay out of this, Smith." He glared at the rustler. "What about it, mister. You feel like answering my question now?"

Sweat poured off the rustler's forehead. He clenched his teeth and shook his head. The young half-breed leaned forward.

"In the name of God, Slade, don't —" Aaron Smith's words were cut off as Slade dropped the butt on the wound again. The rustler screamed and sagged into unconsciousness.

Garth Smith swallowed the rising gorge in his throat and turned away. Joseph Ware wiped at the beads of sweat popping out on his forehead.

Nana poured water over the man's head. Slowly the rustler came around. The defiance had fled his face. His lips bled from where he had chewed them against the pain. "Where's Daughtery taking the herd?"

The rustler's words came in gasps between the pulsating pain that racked his body. "Over to New Mexico Territory. Somewhere around Raton Pass."

"What's Daughtery up to? Why was he headed southwest before he crossed back over the river?"

The wounded man's body stiffened against a wave of excruciating pain. When it passed, he said, "He didn't say nothing to me, but we heard Comancheros was there with Quanah Parker's Comanches, an' I figure he didn't want no truck with them."

The man's words jarred Slade. He glanced up at Nana whose dark eyes flashed his understanding. With Comancheros came whiskey, and with rot-gut whiskey filling their bellies, the Comanches turned meaner than usual.

Slade grimaced. He was going to need a heap of luck for his little outfit to slip through Comanche country undetected. They had their hands full right now without having to fight off a band of Kwahadi Comanches. "What size party they got?"

The rustler shook his head weakly. His face had grown sallow. "I — I don't know. Nobody said. I —"

Slade raised the carbine shoulder high.

"Don't — please, God, don't —," screamed the man. "It's the truth. I don't know."

The young half-breed sat back on his heels, satisfied the wounded rustler had told the truth. He looked over his shoulder in the direction of Palo Duro Canyon. Only a couple days ride separated them from the Comancheros. He hoped the butchers would stay where they were. He had enough trouble with Daughtery and these Mormons.

Slade decided to keep his concern to himself. He gave one last glance in the direction of Palo Duro Canyon before turning his attention back to the rustler. "How long you been with Daughtery?"

"Since last night. Six of us. Six more was to come in today."

A mutter of unrest circulated through the small band of men.

Slade grimaced inwardly. As long as the Mormons had the rustlers vastly outnumbered, they were eager to pursue the herd, but now that the odds had lessened, some of the men might have second thoughts. The only action Slade knew to overcome their sudden apprehensions was to act as if the wounded man's announcement meant nothing to him.

He nodded, and Nana sprinkled a yellow powder on the wound. Moments later, the rustler opened his eyes in amazement. "It don't hurt no more."

Nana tightened the strings about his small bag of medicine and looked at Slade. *"Isatai?"*

Slade's face grew grim. "I hope to hell not."

Joseph Ware spoke up. "What does he

mean, *Isa-tai?*"

The young half-breed and the Apache grinned at each other. Then Slade explained. "*Isa-tai* is the Kwahadi medicine man and just about as important as Quanah Parker himself. *Isa-tai* is mighty respected and looked up to by the young warriors. He gets it in his head to come after us, we got trouble like you've never seen, Joseph."

Nana snorted.

Ware frowned and said to Slade, "Your brother seems to disagree with you."

"He sneers at *Isa-tai,* but he respects the man." Slade paused as Nana spoke rapidly in the Athabaskan dialect. Both grinned, and Slade turned to Ware. "Nana reminded me that the name *Isa-tai* has two or three different meanings. The words are interpreted to mean Little Wolf, which *Isa-tai* prefers."

Slade nodded to his Apache brother. "But we like the other two meanings, the ones that mean Rear End of the Wolf or Coyote Droppings."

Both young men laughed.

Frowning at their laughter, Ware looked from one to the other. "He's dangerous then?"

Slade's laughter faded. "Just hope he doesn't hear that we're around. Quanah is a reasonable man, but old Coyote Droppings is crazier than a mule full of loco weed."

CHAPTER SIXTEEN

Slade asked for two volunteers to take the wounded rustler back to New Gideon. After they rode out, Aaron Smith stepped forward. "How close are we to New Mexico Territory?"

The young half-breed looked around. To the east, the prairie spread to the horizon in gentle, undulating swells covered with shortgrass and sagebrush where it swept up to the flat tableland of the Staked Plains. Still farther to the west, beyond their sight, the plains rolled into the rugged foothills of the Sangre de Cristo Mountains in New Mexico Territory. "Half a day, maybe longer," Slade said.

The elder Smith nodded. "Will we catch them before they reach the territory?"

"I doubt it."

Aaron Smith nodded, his rugged face cut with a deep frown. "As I understand it, Mr. Slade, we are a legal posse at the present.

What will happen if we cross into New Mexico Territory and reclaim our cattle?"

Jake Slade looked over the band of Mormons. In their way, they were good men. A little prejudiced here, a little biased there. That was to be expected. But they did deserve the truth. "So far, we've been legal, but once we reach New Mexico Territory, the legal thing is to contact the federal marshal's office in Santa Fe and ask for his help." He paused, then added. "Which is exactly what we would do if we had the time." He swung onto his saddle.

Aaron Smith stopped Slade. "What you're saying is that we could find ourselves in a peck of trouble with the law by crossing the border and taking our cattle back?"

The young half-breed studied the elder man through narrowed eyes. He had a sinking feeling in the pit of his stomach that everything was fixing to blow up in his face. What the hell, he told himself. The truth's the truth. "We could, Mr. Smith. If we had time, we would do it all nice and legal, but we don't have the time. By the time the marshal gets here, your cows will be boiling in Yankee pots, and Daughtery will be in California."

Smith glanced at the men around him. "I'm a farmer, not a lawman. My crops won't wait. Me and my son are going back to New Gideon. We don't want trouble with the law, especially the federal law."

The elderly man's words stunned Slade even though he had anticipated them. He tried to reason with them. "We're not that far behind your herd. We'll catch them by noon tomorrow."

Aaron Smith shook his head and raised his voice to the crowd. "I don't know about the rest of you, but before I get me and mine afoul of the law, I'll give up my cattle and chalk it up to experience."

Mutters of discord greeted Smith's words. The older man continued. "I'm not saying to forget about our cattle. What I'm saying is that let's take Mr. Slade's suggestion and send one of us to the marshal in Santa Fe. The rest of us can return to New Gideon and get back to our chores."

Several men murmured their approval and sided with the Stake counselor.

Although he understood how they felt, Slade looked on with a mixture of anger and frustration as one after another crossed over to Aaron Smith until only Joseph Ware remained with Slade and Nana.

The young half-breed cleared his throat. "This is what you men want?"

Aaron Smith answered for them. "It is."

Slade shrugged. "I'm going on. Won't be no need for any of you to ride on to Santa Fe. If I don't get your stock, I'll notify the law."

Two or three men grinned.

Slade looked at Joseph Ware and nodded to the men. "Go back with them, Joseph."

The big blacksmith shook his head emphatically. "I'm not quitting. I'm staying. We started out on this together, we can finish it together," he said, glaring at his townsmen, most of whom stared at the ground in embarrassment.

Dismounting and adjusting the cinch on his sorrel, Slade shook his head. "All of us together was one thing. Now, with just me and Nana, we'll handle it different. It'd be too hard on you, believe me," he said. "Besides," he added, glaring at Aaron Smith. "I want someone I can trust to look after Bent back in New Gideon."

Nana sat motionless on his mustang, his face inscrutable.

Joseph Ware understood what Slade was saying, but the logic nevertheless stirred his anger. His blocky jaw set, then relaxed. Slade was right. During the run to the river, the blacksmith had dropped out. And Joseph Ware had the distinct feeling that Slade and Nana's pursuit of the rustlers now

189

would be much more intense than the run to the river. He nodded. "All right."

"But when you leave," Slade said to Ware, pointing downriver, "I want you to circle through that brake of willows and elm along the shore." Smith frowned. Slade explained. "I don't know if we're being watched or not, but I want them to think all of us turned back. Nana and I will drop off in the berry thickets. Then tonight we'll move out."

Later, Slade and Nana watched as the last of the riders disappeared over a sand hill on the horizon. The only sound breaking the silence of the prairie was the soughing of the ever-present wind.

Nana noted the frown on Slade's face. "You are troubled?"

The young half-breed shook his head. "You ever had something just keep worrying you, but you can't figure out what it is?"

Nana misinterpreted his question. "Those men — they do not deserve the cattle."

"I don't mean them. There's something I should know about all this, something that would help, but I can't figure it out." Slade shrugged and hooked a thumb over his shoulder. "One thing I do know though is that someone out there with John Daughtery knows who killed Wiley Bledsoe. I want

190

that someone."

Daughtery pushed the herd harder than Slade figured.

Two days later, as the morning sun cast its orange fingers through the gray mists spreading over the foothills of the Sangre de Cristos, Nana pulled his mustang up beside a scaly-barked ponderosa on the crest of a low promontory and pointed to the valley below them. "There is Daughtery."

The grass was belly high, and the cattle grazed peacefully along a pristine stream that wound its way lazily down the valley through the grama and bluestem. At the edge of an aspen brake on the western side of the valley, campfires issued tendrils of white smoke into the still air. Several men were rolled up in their soogans while others busied themselves around the fires. Unsaddled horses grazed in a rope corral.

Slade reached up and pulled a few pine needles off the ponderosa. He inhaled deeply of the sharp pine scent, and rolled the seven-inch needles between his fingers, crushing them to release even more of the pleasant aroma as he studied the scene below. "Doesn't look to me like they're worried about a posse."

"Maybe they think we all turned back."

"Maybe, maybe not," said Slade. "We can't afford to take the chance that our scheme fooled them. Daughtery gets his hands on us out here, we'll never ride out."

Picketing their animals in some graze in a small box canyon, Slade and Nana returned to the top of the ridge to study the camp from the protection of the ponderosa pines swaying in the breeze. They needed time to decide upon a course of action.

"I count ten," said Slade, frowning at Nana. "That means four are missing."

"Hunting for meat?"

Slade shrugged. "Could be. Could be that jasper lied when he said Daughtery was meeting up with six more yahoos."

After several minutes of studied silence, Nana whispered, "What do you plan?"

The ridge from which they watched rose over a hundred feet above the meadow and made a gradual curve to the end of the valley where it broke off into a broad canyon that cut into the side of the mountain. "We wait and watch," said Slade, his eyes sweeping the bowl-shaped valley before him.

Great, towering pines covered the crest of the slope, so thick that from the distance, the crest appeared a solid blanket of green that rolled down the slope to interweave with the molten gold of aspens, their white bark a sharp contrast against a background of green. Slade pointed to the far side of the valley. "I'll watch from over there. After dark, we'll meet at the canyon at the end of the valley."

Nana agreed, and Slade decided to travel by foot along the crest of the slope and circle the valley by way of the canyon. Fifteen minutes later, he reached the canyon, the sides of which were perpendicular, as straight up and down as the sideboards on a prairie schooner. Unable to descend the vertical cliffs, Slade backtracked and eased down the slope into a thick stand of aspen.

He remained motionless, listening. The only sounds were the distant cries of birds and the wind dancing through the treetops.

Across the valley, a horse whinnied. Slade dropped to one knee beside a slender aspen as another horse nickered. Both animals were looking in his direction. After several moments, they dropped their heads and went back to grazing.

Slade figured the mouth of the canyon to be a quarter of a mile wide. Fortunately the grass was waist high. Slade grunted with satisfaction. At least that was one thing in his favor.

Dropping into a crouch, he left the comfortable protection of the aspen for the uncertain shelter of the waist high grass, angling for the base of the mountain slope on the far side of the canyon. From time to time he paused to peer above the grass. The horses still grazed peacefully.

Just as he reached the mouth of the canyon, a powerful force slammed into his shoulder, spinning him around and sending him sprawling to the ground. In the next instant, the boom of a large bore rifle echoed across the valley. Numbness spread through his shoulder and arm.

He rolled over on his back just as a second slug tore up a chunk of soil the size of his fist where he had been lying. Even before the echo died away, Slade rolled over once again into the tall grass and lay still. Another slug slammed into the ground by his head, and the young half-breed recognized the booming roar of a .52 sliding block Sharps. Without hesitation, he pushed himself to his feet and sprinted for the sanctuary of the canyon as the first wave of excruciating pain drove knives into his shoulder.

Another shot rang out, and a 410-grain slug smashed into the ground at his feet. His brain reeled, trying to push the pain aside long enough to figure out just where the gunman had hidden himself.

Two more shots whistled past his ears before he reached the canyon and ducked behind a large boulder. He grimaced against the searing pain, at the same time cursing himself for being so careless. Quickly he checked his shoulder. The slug had gouged out a ragged wound in his deltoid muscle, missing the bone. The wound was clean, but bleeding profusely. Sweat popped out on his forehead as he packed his neckerchief over his shoulder. He'd have to worry about it later. Right now, he had to light a shuck out of there.

Another shot rang out, and a slug splattered against a rock at his feet. He scanned the rim of the canyon. All he knew was that the gunman was somewhere above him. But where?

Gritting his teeth against the pain, he zigzagged down the canyon, which cut sharply to the right. He didn't know where it led, but he had no choice. He had to follow the canyon and hope that he could find a hiding place quick.

The men in the camp must have heard the shots. They would be here within minutes. Around the next bend, the canyon forked. His chest heaving, Slade paused to catch his breath. His shoulder throbbed.

A faint shout reached his ears, and then he felt the ground vibrating from the pounding of hooves. He looked around. Behind him, like a chimney, a narrow fissure in the granite walls angled upward to the top of the canyon.

He threw his hat on the ground at the base of the fissure, then dashed down the right fork of the canyon, taking care to keep to the rocks so there would be no footprints in the sand. He stopped abruptly at a granite slab that had fallen from the canyon walls and landed at an oblique angle against the perpendicular wall. The slab reminded Slade of one of the cattle ramps at the railhead at Dodge. At the top of the ramp was a narrow ledge about fifteen feet above the ground.

Behind him the sound of hoofbeats grew louder. It's better than nothing, he told himself, backing up for a run at the granite slab. He reached the top, and then managed to pull himself over the ledge where he pressed himself into the rock.

Seconds later, horses pounded past. Voices shouted and cursed. Then a voice Slade recognized as Ed Towers' cut through the confusion. "Back here. I found his hat."

Although Slade could not hear their conversation, he knew that they were studying the fissure. If he was lucky, they would figure that he had climbed the fracture to the top of the canyon.

Long seconds passed, and then the canyon erupted with retreating hoofbeats as the riders spurred their horses to reach the top of the canyon before their quarry.

Slade stumbled down from the ledge and, cradling his arm to his chest to alleviate some of the pain, headed up the twisting canyon, which grew narrow as it ascended the mountain. He felt blood and sweat trickling down his side.

From time to time, distant shouts echoed from the pine forests off to his right. He had to find shelter. He didn't worry about Nana. By now, the Apache and the horses were miles away. After dusk, Nana would picket the horses and return. So now, Slade's only task was to find a hiding place, tend his wound, and wait.

Around the next bend, the canyon opened onto a pine-choked ravine. Without hesitation, Slade disappeared into the ravine, along the bottom of which wound a narrow bed of sand, dry now, but mute evidence of the runoff from the melting snow high above. Dead pine needles lay in the sand. He took care not to step in the soft ground. He scanned the banks of the sandy bed anxiously as he fled down the ravine. The shouts of the rustlers faded in the distance.

Suddenly, he spotted what he had been looking for. In a broad bend in the ravine, the runoff water had cut several feet back under the roots of a chokeberry thicket, leaving a hollow less than eighteen inches high. Thick strands of grass hung over the opening.

After poking a long stick inside to make sure he would have the hollow all to himself, Slade built a pile of pine needles and gathered a handful of cobwebs and crawled inside. The pine needles he had cast onto the sandy bed to cover his tracks, and the cobweb he used to plug the hole in his shoulder.

He lay back on the sand and closed his eyes to the throbbing pain shooting through his body. He had been a white man too long, he told himself angrily. He found it difficult to block the pain from his thoughts. He should have remained with the Apache. Their ways, although not understood by the white man, were good.

The pain began to subside as Slade forced his thoughts back to his days as a youth with the Apache. Soon he dozed.

It was dark when he awakened. Perspiration had soaked his clothes. He shivered.

Fever from the wound. He curled into a ball, hoping to contain as much body heat as possible. The remainder of the night was a nightmare of feverish sleep and shivering wakefulness.

Just after false dawn, Slade slipped out of his cave and backtracked up the ravine, guessing that the rustlers would be looking for him to head into the foothills away from the canyon. His shoulder throbbed with each step. Within seconds, sweat beaded on his forehead. He tried to force the pain from his mind by planning on his next course of action.

Higher up the mountain, he could find shelter and build a small fire. Then he could worry about food. He knew that Nana would be searching for him. Suddenly he stumbled to a halt, his pain-racked eyes fixed on a tangled green vine clinging to a dead pine at the edge of a clearing — wild clematis. In the summer, the vine had a beautiful red bloom, shaped like a narrow-necked clay pot.

He crushed a handful of leaves in his hand and pressed them into the bullet wound. The leaves stung, but he felt an astringent, tightening sensation as the healing liquids seeped into his wound.

After stripping the remainder of the leaves

and shoving them in his vest pocket, he popped several bare stalks into his mouth and chewed on them. He shuddered at the bitter taste, but forced himself to continue chewing. The white meat beneath the skin would drive away the fever.

His steps seemed lighter as he resumed his journey up the mountain. The clematis would dull the pain even as it healed the wound.

Midmorning, Slade found his sanctuary, a cleft in the granite mountain that took a sharp turn just inside the entrance. He peered into the darkness at what seemed to be a large room. Quickly he built a small fire from dried wood. He was right. The room was the size of a barn. In the middle of the room lay the remains of ancient fires, ashes that had turned to dust and had been spread by scurrying rodents and slithering snakes.

Using a burning brand, he made his way deeper into the cave, noting how the tip of the flame curled to the rear of the cave. That was good. Any smoke from his fire would dissipate by the time it reached the surface.

He stuck the torch into a rift in the wall and returned to the entrance to erase signs of his fire and gather fuel. Wood was plentiful. Soon he had a cheery fire blazing. The heat soaked into his lanky body, driving the chill away as he tended his wound with fresh medication.

He licked his parched lips and gathered saliva in his mouth for his dry throat. He needed water — and food, he told himself as hunger pangs growled in his stomach. "I'll rest a spell, then I'll go dig up something," he muttered, lying back on the hard floor, soaking up the comforting warmth of the fire.

Moments later, he fell into a deep slumber.

Outside, riders scoured the mountainside searching for the young half-breed. One pulled up and sniffed the air. "Ain't that wood smoke?"

The second rider sniffed. "That's from our place."

"I don't think so. We're camped way down in the valley."

"So what? The way the wind blows through these hills an' all, the smoke might be coming all the way from Santa Fe."

The first rider laughed and continued on down the mountain.

CHAPTER SEVENTEEN

The fire had burned to embers when Slade awakened. He stirred the coals and fed fresh tinder to the blinking red spots. A tiny flame erupted and quickly grew into a small blaze.

He rose to his feet, gingerly touching his shoulder. He winced. The pain was still there, but he knew just how quickly the clematis healed. His stomach growled, and he ran his tongue over his parched lips.

Time to tend the body now, he told himself, making his way from the firelight into the mouth of the cave. Water and food would be easy to find in the Sangre de Cristos.

Outside the sun was rising. He had almost slept the clock around. Far above, a granite ledge jutted out from the side of the mountain, an ideal overlook to scan the country for any visitors.

On the way up to the ledge, Slade dug roots and herbs to fill his stomach. Just below the ledge, he found a tiny pool of crystal clear water, cold and sweet. He filled his belly. He ate some more roots, but meat was what he craved, broiled meat.

Later, he lay on the granite ledge soaking up the blazing sun, feeling very indolent and very Indian, but still very hungry. There was nothing to do. Slade had considered building a signal fire for Nana, but decided to wait for at least a day. Daughtery might have left some men behind. The bearded man was too smart not to know the identity of the man they pursued. Anyone could recognize Slade's battered slouch hat.

But Slade doubted if the men would maintain the search for more than a day or two, and this was the second day.

As he lay in the sun, his thoughts drifted back to the murder of Wiley Bledsoe. Suddenly, the elusive worry that had nagged at him blossomed to life, but just as quickly evaporated like a wisp of smoke.

A soft scraping sound reached his ears. He turned his head and grinned. Here came the meat he had been craving in the form of a mountain rattler, drawn by curiosity to the inert figure it smelled on the ledge.

The rattlesnake coiled and flicked its tongue, testing the air. Slade rose and headed for the rear of the ledge. There he cut a forked limb and casually pinned the rattler to the ground while he lopped off its head. He gutted it and headed back to the cave, pausing at the pool of water for another long drink.

Back in the cave, the wiry young man tended his wound while chunks of rattlesnake broiled and sizzled on spits.

Suddenly a muted gunshot reached his ears.

Moving quickly, he made his way to the cave entrance.

Three riders were coming up the mountain directly toward the cave. Were they aware of its existence? Or was this all part of a random search? Slade reached for his revolver.

Though they were too distant for Slade to make out their words, he could tell from their gesticulating that they were arguing whether to continue their search up the mountain or return to the valley. When they were less than a hundred yards from the cave entrance, they halted. Slade recognized one of the men — Ed Towers.

Suddenly Slade thought of the broiling meat inside. Would the riders smell it?

Ed Towers fished in his pocket and pulled out a bag of makings. Deftly, he rolled a cigarette and tossed the bag to one of the other riders as he struck a match. Slade grinned. The cigarette smoke would cover any other smell.

The burly foreman inhaled deeply and blew out a stream of smoke and pointed to the foothills and turned his horse around. The other two looked at each other, and then with a shrug turned to follow Daughtery's foreman.

Slade breathed a sigh of relief.

Suddenly a voice above his head said, "You always had luck."

The young half-breed jumped back into the cave, and then relaxed as he recognized the voice of his Apache brother. He holstered his revolver as Nana swung down from where he had been hiding above the cave entrance. "That's a good way to pick up a couple ounces of lead."

Nana just grinned, and Slade motioned for him to follow.

While they ate, Nana brought Slade up to date. Daughtery and his band had moved out fast, pushing the cattle hard, hard enough to be in Raton Pass within three days. The Apache paused. "The arm is hurt?"

"It's healing," replied Slade, noting earlier how Nana's eyes kept going back to the young half-breed's shoulder. "I reckon I can fork a horse tomorrow. The trail will be easy to follow."

"Good. I will find us food to carry on our journey," said Nana, wiping the snake grease from his lips with his fingers and running them through his long black hair as he rose from his squat.

Early next morning, the two rode out with Nana in the lead, a deer haunch tied on each side of his saddle. The Apache maintained a steady pace, pausing regularly to give Slade's wound a rest. But by noon, the throbbing wound had begun to bleed.

"It is no problem," said Nana when Slade protested their stopping. "We have made up much time on the herd." He removed the bandage and sprinkled yellow monkey flower on the wound. "Now we rest and eat. You make the fire, and I cut the meat."

While the venison steaks broiled on spits, Nana shaved the remainder of the haunches into thin slices and draped them over the limbs of nearby bushes to begin the drying process in the blazing sun.

He then squatted by the small fire and reached into his medicine bag. He pulled out a handful of dried, spade-shaped petals, all wrinkled and twisted. He handed one to Slade. "Peyote," he said simply.

Slade chewed on the drug, relishing the

numbing warmth that drove away the pain in his shoulder. As the pain fled, his hunger returned with a vengeance. He devoured his steak and half of Nana's and drank a copious amount of water after which he lay back in the sun and closed his eyes.

Nana nodded with satisfaction when his brother's breathing became deep and regular. Rising to his feet, he disappeared into the pine and aspen forest in search of roots and herbs. In a nearby valley, he dug mudwater plantain from the edge of a small pond. To him, the plantain tasted no different from the Indian potato. The Apache studied the plantain, unsure just what was in these roots to still the hunger pangs in a man's stomach that even fresh venison could not assuage.

He knew from experience that plantain eaten with meat gave much strength. He grunted. Now his brother would have his hunger satisfied. But Slade also needed energy, which Nana supplied by gathering a parfleche bag full of pine nuts.

When Slade awakened, sliced venison broiled by the fire while baked plantains steamed and pine nuts roasted in the coals. In a bark bowl, tea steeped from the twigs of wild berries gave off a faint and delicate aroma. As Slade looked on, Nana dropped another hot rock in the bowl.

After the meal, Slade checked his shoulder. The skin was pink and healthy, and he almost believed that he could see the wound closing. He applied another poultice of yellow monkey flower and wild clematis to his shoulder. He felt like riding out, but he knew better, and he also knew that any delay could more than be made up with the extra strength gained by another night's rest.

They rode out the next morning before sunup, halting periodically to give his wound a rest. As the day progressed, time between rest periods increased until the second day. Slade rode from midafternoon until dusk without the wound reopening.

Around the small fire that night, Slade said, "Looks like we'll catch them about the time they hit Raton Pass." He sliced a chunk of venison and popped it in his mouth. "You and me'll be dancing around like painted ladies if we try to take that herd back to New Gideon by our lonesomes."

The Apache grunted. "It is wise that you see such." There was an undertone of teasing in his voice.

Arching an eyebrow, Slade replied in kind. "I am not a foolish rabbit. Perhaps I do not have the mind of the fox as my brother seems to think he has, but I manage to

208

reach my wickiup every night."

Nana grinned at the subtle sarcasm. "What would you have us do?"

"We circle around them tonight and wait at the settlement at Raton Pass. They will sell the animals, and we will take them and the money back to New Gideon."

For several moments, Nana worried over the idea. Finally he shook his head. "I do not like it."

Slade frowned. "Why?"

"How do we know they will come to Raton Pass?"

"Where else could they go?"

Nana shrugged. He did not like the plan. He did not want to let the rustlers out of sight. Much could go wrong, a feeling he expressed to Slade.

"What could happen? They have to sell the herd in Raton. That's the only place around, and we'll be waiting for them when they leave town. We waylay them, then head back to Texas with them."

Nana spoke with misgiving in his voice. "That is like the spider that waits in his hole. Perhaps his prey will pass by. Perhaps it will not. Perhaps it will fight. Perhaps it will not. No, we should be like the hawk watching the rabbit below. He sees where the rabbit runs, then he follows."

"All right," said Slade testily. "Then you tell me what we should do."

Nana ignored the annoyance in Slade's voice. "We are Apache. We follow and watch. Then as the hawk, we will open our talons when the time is right."

Slade glared at his Apache brother who stared back at him innocently with an almost imperceptible trace of a smile on his lips. Damn those Apaches and their poker faces, Slade grumbled to himself. But, the truth of the matter was that Nana's suggestion did make more sense than his own.

He relaxed and grinned. Hell, Nana had always been the one with the cooler head, even as boys in swing kicking, a violent game in which Apache boys fought with their feet. The last boy on his feet was declared the winner.

More than once, Slade lost his temper, only to receive a bloody nose or a split lip from one of his brothers, Nana or Paleto. "All right. We'll do it your way. We sleep tonight and watch them tomorrow."

The night passed quickly. They rode out before dawn, and at noon, they spied the stolen cattle, which the rustlers were still pushing, but not as hard as they had a few days earlier. By midafternoon, Slade and Nana rode the ridges high above the herd.

Slade counted eleven men, three of whom rode drag. After thirty minutes of watching, he nodded to the men in the rear. "They must figure they got away clean."

Nana grunted. He saw as Slade. The rustlers never bothered to check over their shoulders. They had nothing to fear from behind.

As Slade watched, John Daughtery and Ed Towers rode up to the point. Daughtery motioned to the herd, and the point man began circling the cattle. Slade frowned. It was too early to stop.

Nana pointed north beyond the next pine-covered ridge. Several columns of smoke rose into the still air. The settlement at Raton Pass. They had reached their destination.

Dismounting, Slade said, "After dark, we'll move in closer. We don't want to lose anybody. I figure Daughtery will ride into Raton in the morning. We'll be waiting for him."

As the sun set behind the mountains and the shadows fell cold and black across the valley, Slade leaned back against a pine and chewed on a piece of venison. He scooted around, trying to find a spot where the scaly bark was smoothest.

"The moon will be half-empty tonight."

The wiry young man glanced at Nana. "I know."

Nana nodded to the valley. "It will be darkest before the moon rises."

"That's when we'll make our move," Slade replied, his lean face impassive.

Darkness filled the valley, and like a bowl of black water, rose to overflow the mountain peaks. "It is time," said Slade, tightening the cinch on the sorrel.

Slowly they picked their way down the mountainside. Moving as silently as possible, Slade and Nana rode to the Raton side of the valley, taking care to stay just inside the forest. There they would await John Daughtery and Ed Towers. Slade felt a sense of satisfaction.

Slade awakened early, and, from his vantage point in the forest, watched as the rustlers' camp slowly came to life.

Banked fires were stirred and fed, coffee was put on. As the camp moved about, Slade became concerned. Where was Daughtery and Towers? He studied the camp carefully, but the two men had disappeared.

Moments later, the rattle of a buckboard sounded from behind. Slade glanced around as a well-dressed man in a gray suit, silk vest, and black bowler emerged from the pines in a buckboard pulled by matching bays. Slade watched curiously as the buckboard clattered into the rustlers' camp, figuring that Daughtery or Ed Towers would meet the buckboard, but neither was in the group awaiting the approaching wagon.

A sinking feeling knotted Slade's stomach as the man spoke with one of the rustlers, handed him a small package, pointed toward Raton Pass, and then turned the buckboard around and headed back in the direction from which he had come.

Slade had permitted the businessman to ride in, but he and Nana blocked the road when the man tried to ride out of the valley. The portly businessman's eyes grew wide at the sight of the Apache.

The young half-breed heeled his sorrel up to the side of the buckboard. "Where's John Daughtery?" The ice in his voice matched the chill in his gray eyes.

The man gulped and his tongue darted out to wet his lips as he saw Nana slowly withdraw his double-edged knife.

Without taking his eyes from the Apache, the portly man replied so hastily that his words stumbled over each other. "Raton Pass. H-he's back in Raton Pass. He came in right after dark last night."

"What are you doing out here?"

Without hesitation, the man answered. "I — I'm a cattle buyer. I purchased the herd from him. I — I — ah —" His corpulent body shuddered, and his terror-filled eyes fluttered shut. "Please, don't kill me. I haven't done anything."

"Nobody plans on doing anything if you tell me what I want to know. Now, what's your business out here?"

The shaken man forced his eyes open. "To give the men their wages and directions to my place," he blubbered.

"What about John Daughtery? Where is he?"

"I don't know. I don't know. Believe me. I paid him for the herd last night. He asked me to bring the wages out to his riders this morning. Honest. That's all I know."

His face burning with frustration, Slade glanced at his Apache brother. He should have known not to count on Daughtery doing the expected. Without a word, the two men wheeled about and headed for Raton Pass.

Throughout the thirty-minute ride to the mountain village, Slade berated himself for letting Daughtery slip through his fingers. Putting a rope on the damned man was like trying to herd cats. Just before they reached

214

Raton Pass, a gray curtain of rain rolled down the mountain, forcing the two to take shelter under a granite ledge.

Within minutes, water coursed down the wagon ruts in the road, washing away all sign. After the shower passed, Slade headed into Raton Pass, leaving Nana behind in the forest.

Daughtery was not to be found in the small town, but in the Lodgepole Saloon, Slade found Ed Towers. The hulking foreman had a laugh on his face, a half-empty bottle in his hand, and a burly arm curled around one of the local crib girls. The discordant sounds of the piano echoed Towers' raucous laughter.

The foreman's laughter froze in his throat when he spied Slade push through the batwings. For several moments, Ed Towers stood rooted to the wooden floor. The drunken hilarity faded from his eyes as they narrowed into malevolent black slits. The girl on his arm glanced around, puzzled, wondering what had jerked the wild celebration up short. A frown darkened her face when she saw Slade slip the loop off the hammer of his .44.

A sneer curled Towers' thick lips. He pushed the girl aside and tossed the bottle over his shoulder, shattering it against the floor.

Slowly the low grumble of voices and music faded as one saloon patron after another, from swillpot to banker, from dilettante to harlot, became aware of the two men facing each other. Two or three revelers stepped forward so they could hear the exchange.

Ed Towers jeered. "Well, look what we got here. Just what the hell do you think you're doin' in a white man's saloon, Injun boy?" Slowly he dropped his hand to his side.

Chapter Eighteen

Slade remained motionless, his eyes fastened on Towers. "Where's Daughtery?"

Towers laughed with a mocking sneer. "Go to hell."

The lanky man shrugged. "Makes no difference to me. You or him — one of you will tell me what I want to know."

"Don't count on it, sonny." Towers bent his knees and leaned forward. His gun arm tensed.

A faint smile turned up the edges of Slade's thin lips. With casual aplomb, he said, "You'll be dead before you clear leather."

Towers snarled and glared at Slade, but the amused look in the younger man's eyes unnerved him. A sudden fear filled the foreman's chest. He swallowed hard.

Slade's smile remained fixed on his lips. "Who killed Wiley Bledsoe?"

The saloon grew silent. The crowd, suddenly realizing the drama unfolding before them, pulled back, leaving the two men alone in the middle of the room.

Ed Towers searched the saloon desperately for aid. But as his eyes touched those of other saloon patrons, they looked away. No one moved to his support.

"I'll ask you once more, Towers. Who killed Wiley Bledsoe?"

Abruptly, Towers' face grew hard. He narrowed his eyes and clenched his teeth. "Go to hell," he hissed. "I ain't tellin' you nothing."

Slade took a step forward. "Then I'll beat it out of you."

Before Slade's words had died away, Ed Towers' hand streaked for his revolver.

But Slade was faster. In one blazing blur, his .44 leaped into his hand, belching orange flames from the muzzle.

Towers stiffened, the muzzle of his .45 still in the holster. He stared at Slade in disbelief, then dropped his eyes to the spreading red stain on his chest. He tugged on his revolver, but it had grown too heavy to move. He tried to step forward, but a great weariness filled his body. His muscles grew rubbery. With a jar, he dropped to his knees, his arms limp at his side. He opened his mouth to speak, but instead of words, blood trickled from his lips. With a groan, he fell forward, dead before his bearded face smashed into the sawdust-covered floor.

"I saw it," shouted a fence post of a man rushing forward. "He drew first. It was self-defense."

Several well-wishers crowded in to clap Slade on the back and offer to buy him a beer.

He dropped his .44 into its holster and asked of the skinny man, "Where's the law around here."

A man in a black suit pushed through the crowd. "Ain't none," the man said, kneeling to check the body. "I'm the undertaker," he added after turning the body over and laying his hand on Towers' chest. "Heard the shot. Figured I might be needed." He continued talking as he went through Towers' pockets. "Never seen this jasper hereabouts before. I bury them what got no family for whatever I find on them. I —"

His words lodged in his throat as he pulled out a wad of bills from Towers' shirt pocket. He whistled softly as he rose and counted the money. He looked at Slade. "There's over a hundred dollars here."

Slade ran his fingers through his short-cut hair and grinned. "I'd say that after you buy a round for the house, that should make your day." With that, he left the saloon.

Across the dirt street was a sutler. The young half-breed purchased a new hat with reluctance. They were all stiff and hard, not like his comfortable old slouch hat he had lost back in the canyon. But a hat was a necessity whether in the mountains or on the plains, at least it was if he didn't want to bake his brains or let the wind blow them out his ears.

After the sutler, Slade headed for the livery. The bowlegged old man who owned the stable remembered Daughtery. "Yep, he swapped off that dun over yonder for a spanking fine bay. Fact is," he added in a whining voice as his eyes played over the sorrel Slade rode, "I figure he done got the best of me on the trade. Once upon a time, I was a good haggler, but age done creeped up on me. I been losing my shirt on ever' deal I made of late."

Slade glanced over the old man's head. The livery was full of slick-looking animals that could fool most. But no amount of grooming could hide the telltale signs from the Nez Perce in Slade. With a practiced eye, he spotted the ringworm scars, observed the large chest and pot belly of heaves, and noted the opaque corneas of moonblindness.

"He headed north of here," the old man said. "You be headin' after him, you need yourself a sound animal — not," he added hastily, "not that your sorrel ain't sound, but it appears he's been ridden hard the last few days. A fresh animal would sure be a boon."

"No, thanks." Slade eyed the livery again, nodded to the old man, and rode out.

Kansas Jack squatted on his heels by the campfire, sipping whiskey-laced Arbuckle coffee from a battered tin cup. He squinted his eyes against the smoke as he studied the cowpoke standing on the other side of the fire. "He got Ed, you say?"

The cowboy nodded. "Saw it myself, Jack. That breed's faster than a snake."

Jack scratched the stubble on his jaw. "Always figgered Ed would bully the wrong jasper sooner or later." His lips curled into a cruel grin. "I'd say it served him right." He set his cup on the ground and pulled out a bag of Bull Durham and began building a cigarette. "Fast, you say."

Shaking his head, the cowpoke grunted, "Yep."

"Fast as me?"

A crooked grin played over the lean cowpoke's face. "I'd sure hate to live on the dif-

221

ference."

Kansas Jack grinned. So Slade was alive like Daughtery had surmised back at the bluff. Well, for the time being, he would be hot on Daughtery's trail. That gave Kansas Jack time to tie up loose ends and hightail it out of the state just in case Slade decided to come after him for his part in the rustling.

He picked up a small branch from the fire to light his cigarette and glanced around the camp at the other cowpokes rolling out their soogans for the night. Might as well take care of the first loose end now. "Where's the kid, Joe — Rearden, I think his name is — where's he at?" He tossed the burning branch back into the fire and picked up his coffee.

The cowboy shrugged. "Said he wuz tired of the owlhoot trail. He took his share and cut out."

Kansas Jack stood abruptly, his eyes narrowing. "Where to?"

"Who knows? To start over somewhere, I reckon. Why? What's the trouble? He wasn't that much of a hand noway."

Angrily, the outlaw slung the dregs of his cup on the fire and jammed the cigarette between his lips. He puffed furiously. The kid was weak, and he knew enough to hang them all.

Kansas Jack had lied when he promised Daughtery he wouldn't hurt the boy. He should have taken care of the kid as soon as Daughtery and Towers pulled out, but he had figured he would have time after his men got back from Raton Pass with supplies.

He cursed himself for the blunder. Well, he made himself a promise he would sure keep this time. He wouldn't blunder again. He would find Joe Rearden, and he would kill the kid. Then there would be no weak links.

Slade and Nana skirted Raton Pass and cut the northern road two miles outside of the small settlement. Thirty minutes later, Nana grunted and pointed to the ground. "Maybe he smart like the white man, but the Apache could teach him of horses."

"No," said Slade. "Daughtery knows horses. I think he just got careless."

Nana pointed to the tracks. The animal was beginning to favor the front right. The edges of the tracks were sharp and crisp in the mud. "Look."

"I see them." Slade looked up the road, trying to see beyond the horizon. "I think he's made the mistake we've been hoping for." Nana frowned as Slade explained, "All

223

the horses in the livery back in Raton Pass were worn-out. Daughtery just got in too big of a hurry to pick out the best from a herd of throwaways." The leather-tough young half-breed studied the tracks. "I figure he's less than an hour ahead."

The Apache brave glanced at Slade. "Gokhlayeh always said you had eyes of the Apache."

Slade grinned and kicked the sorrel into a running walk.

A few miles farther, the road forked. Daughtery had taken the road to the left. "Looks like he's heading for Denver," Slade mumbled as his eyes followed the sign up the narrow road that clung precipitously to the side of the mountain. A twenty-foot-wide fender of talus lined the edge of the road, debris shoved aside during construction.

Nana grunted. "The horse will not last the day. Already, we have gained much."

"Fine with me. The sooner we hog-tie him and get him and the money back to New Gideon, the better I'll like it."

"It would be easier to just take the money back."

Slade looked at Nana whose eyes remained on the road ahead. He was right. It would be easier. But — "He can tell us about Wiley Bledsoe."

"I know," Nana said, nodding. "What about Bent? We have been many days from village of the Mormons."

"I've thought about him, too. But I trust Joseph Ware. He promised to take care of Bent. I believe him." He glanced at Nana.

The Apache frowned.

"You don't believe Ware will help?"

"I trust the word of no white man."

"I am white."

"You are half-white."

"Does that mean you only believe half of what I say?" Slade teased him.

"No. I believe all. The Indian half will not let white half tell lies."

Slade grinned at his brother's serious reply. "Why is it the Apache looks down upon the white man, thinks that he is much better?" He knew the answer, but he always enjoyed joshing Nana.

"The Apache is the child of the Spirit. The Apache is real human being." Nana tore his eyes from the road and glared at Slade. "Why you ask? You know answer. You sat with me when Mangas told us such."

Slade shrugged. His grin broadened. "I just like for you to remind me."

Dark clouds rolled over the line of mountain peaks to the north. The faraway rumble of thunder sounded like distant drums. Then silence gripped the mountains.

Slade shivered.

The whinny of a horse split the still air. Both men reined up just as a rifle boomed.

CHAPTER NINETEEN

A slug tore out a chunk of bark from a pine next to Slade. Had he not pulled up when he did, his head would have taken the slug.

He threw himself from his horse and drew his revolver all in one motion, landing among scattered bucket-sized granite boulders. His wrist struck a sharp edge on one of the boulders, numbing his hand and sending his revolver skittering down the mantle of rock lining the road.

The rifle boomed again. A rock exploded near his head, peppering the crown of his hat with needle sharp shards of granite. Leaping to his feet, he sprinted several steps and lunged for the protection of a giant pine. He hit and rolled over a bed of sharp rocks, striking his still tender shoulder against the corner of one. Waves of pain shot through his body. He shook his head against the darkness threatening to overcome him.

To his left, on the other side of the road, a

227

second rifle roared. It was Nana with his battered Winchester. Struggling to a sitting position, Slade leaned against the pine, drawing deep breaths, filling his lungs with head-clearing gulps of fresh air.

For several moments, Slade listened to the exchange of gunfire. Nana's shots indicated that the Apache was moving, but the bushwacker's all came from the same spot. Slade peered around the pine. Movement up the slope caught his eye. Daughtery. The rustler was in clear sight.

Slade groaned in frustration. If only he had his sidearm. He looked around. The revolver lay on the talus less than ten feet distant.

Rising into a crouch, Slade eased backward, taking care to keep the tree between him and Daughtery. The revolver lay outside the corridor of protection offered by the pine. And at some point Slade knew that he would have to step beyond that shelter.

He paused. Only two arms'-length distant, the .44 glittered in the sunlight. Slowly, he extended his arm, hoping Daughtery would miss the movement.

A slug slammed into the rocks inches from his wrist. Pieces and slivers of exploding rock stung his arm. He yanked it back and remained motionless.

The forest grew silent. There was no sound other than the rustle of pine needles high overhead. Slade strained for the slightest noise, a scratch of feet in dirt, the clink of metal against rock, anything to indicate what Daughtery was up to.

High above on the mountain, a branch cracked. No animal. The gunfire would have already spooked them out of the area. Either someone drawn by the gunfire, or maybe only a dead limb falling.

Slowly Slade eased back to the pine as the roll of thunder echoed across the valley.

Seconds later, he heard what he had been listening for. A boot scraped against a rock. Daughtery was moving, which also meant that the rancher was probably trying to get into a spot where he could see Slade. In all probability, the rancher had his eyes on the last place he had seen the young half-breed.

Where in the hell was Nana? Surely, Daughtery hadn't hit the Apache. But even if Nana was unhurt, Slade couldn't wait around. At this very moment, the rustler was probably working his way into a better position. Slade picked up a rock the size of a tin cup.

He hurled the rock as far down the mountain as he could. He bunched his legs and fixed his eyes on the .44. Ten feet beyond the .44 was another pine. That's where he was headed.

When he heard the rock hit and clatter against other rocks, Slade burst from behind the pine and raced across the clearing. "Where in the hell is that damned Indian when I need him," he muttered to himself as he scooped up the revolver without missing a step.

Just as he threw himself behind the second pine, a boom ripped the silence apart, and a slug ripped a chunk out of the pine.

Nana's Winchester cracked from above Slade. When Daughtery returned the fire, Slade broke down the mountainside, his moccasined feet flying over the pine needles faster than a cat's over hot rocks. The jarring of his feet sent spasms of pain through his shoulder.

Thirty yards down the slope, he discovered a fissure in the granite that slashed upward at an oblique angle, coming out above Daughtery.

Slade dropped into the cleft. A cool breeze touched the sweat on his head. Dark clouds scudded across the valley, spreading ominous shadows over the forest. The wind picked up, hurling dust and leaves into his eyes. Thunder boomed overhead.

The gunfire continued. Slade made his

way up the rift, which grew shallow as it ascended the mountain. The young half-breed was forced to crawl on his hands and knees to remain out of sight. From the sound of the firing, he had moved above and behind Daughtery.

Great streaks of lightning stabbed down from the black clouds. Zigzag streaks of white fire slashed dizzying patterns across the sky. The wind intensified. A strange tingling spread through his body. He dropped to the bottom of the fracture as a bolt of lightning exploded less than ten feet from him, deafening him. Seconds later, another explosion shook the ground.

Slade lay motionless, dazed by the concussion, his ears ringing. The smell of burning sulfur filled the air. Moments later, the acrid odor of wood smoke stung his nostrils, and the crackle of leaping flames cut through the ringing in his ears.

Shaking his head to clear the cobwebs, he peered over the rim of the shallow fracture. A line of flames raced up the mountain, driven to towering heights by the swirling wind. The roar of the fire reminded him of one of those six-wheeled wood-burning locomotives that began crisscrossing the middle of the country the year before.

Thick smoke engulfed Slade, burning his

throat and stinging his eyes. Blindly, he stumbled back down the fracture. The heat grew intense. Below, the fissure cut back under the granite, a safe refuge from the searing flames. He glanced at the raging conflagration racing up the mountainside with the roar of a locomotive. Could he reach the overhang before the flames leaped the fissure?

Stumbling down the crevice, he strained his eyes against the stinging smoke. Sparks struck his bare skin, singed his hair, and the roar of the flames filled his ears. He could go no farther. He fell to his stomach in the fissure and folded his arms over his head.

A nightmare of heat and flames swept past, dropping sparks that quickly burned through his shirt and blistered his flesh. Moments later, the roar of the fire died away as it swept up the slope, hurled upward by the violent updrafts created by the heat. He leaped to his feet, slapping at his smoldering garments.

Above, a thick mantle of smoke and the stinging smell of turpentine enveloped the mountain. Pines exploded as the intense heat set the resin to boiling, sending hissing flames and black smoke billowing into the sky. The hungry firestorm savagely ate its way through the pines like a starving wolf ravaging a tiny cottontail.

And somewhere in the whirlwind of destruction climbing the mountain was Nana. Slade clenched his teeth. He knew that Nana could take care of himself, but he couldn't help worrying.

Behind Slade, a dark curtain of rain approached from across the valley. Within minutes, a driving rainstorm soaked the mountainside. The raging flames protested, hissed, sputtered; burning logs snapped and cracked; but the rain continued unabated.

Slade stumbled on down the fissure and slipped under the granite slab overhanging it.

After an hour, the rain moved on, dragging the overcast sky with it. Slade trudged up the mountain and into the burn, figuring that Daughtery had escaped during the fire. Tendrils of smoke rose from charred timber. Some stumps still burned, the pitch-soaked wood impervious to the rain. Almost a square mile of mountainside had been devastated.

As he expected, Slade found no sign of Daughtery. If the rustler fled ahead of the fire, Nana should have spotted him. Slade reached the road and backtracked toward Raton Pass. Around the first bend, he found his sorrel lying on its side between two smoldering pines on a nearby knoll.

He winced as he read the sign. The sorrel had panicked and run into the forest where the saddle became entangled in low limbs. A .44 slug would have been much less painful.

He touched his toe to his saddle. It was beyond salvage as was his other gear, his saddle gun, his bow, his soogan.

The sound of a whippoorwill drifted across the blackened mountainside. Slade looked up. Beyond the burn, Nana raised his hand.

The Apache was studying the road when Slade reached him. One glance told the young half-breed all he needed to know. "I'll be damned," he muttered.

During the confusion of the fire, John Daughtery had stumbled upon Nana's horse. The rain had washed out most of the tracks, but there was enough evidence to indicate that the rancher had headed back to Raton Pass.

A light scud of clouds blew across the cold face of the waning moon as they set up camp a couple miles north of Raton Pass. "Snow comes," said Nana.

Slade glanced at the rapidly moving clouds. He had never been able to read the weather with the same degree of certainty as Nana so he had learned to trust his brother's predictions. "Soon?"

"A few days."

"I'll go into the settlement at Raton Pass early in the morning for horses and see if I can find out what happened to Daughtery."

"You have money?"

"I reckon enough to get us a couple ponies that we won't have to carry too far," he replied, remembering the sad condition of the animals at the livery.

Nana dug into the sash supporting his loincloth. He handed Slade a gold nugget. "Buy ones that we do not have to carry."

With a grin, Slade pocketed the nugget and stretched out beside the small fire.

He returned the next morning riding bareback on a buckskin and leading a gray.

Nana arched an eyebrow as he studied his new horse.

"These were his best. Cost all we had."

A sardonic grin revealed Nana's even white teeth as his black eyes swept over the animals, quickly evaluating their conformation and soundness. "And the white man calls the Indian a thief."

Slade laughed and tossed the rope to Nana who deftly looped a lark's head knot around the gray's lower jaw and swung onto the animal's back. "Daughtery caught the evening stage for Santa Fe. We should catch up with him before nightfall."

They picked up the road south of Raton Pass. Two hours later, Slade pulled up at the edge of the forest, overlooking a broad meadow in the middle of which sprawled a relay station and its corrals. He preferred avoiding all the stations, but he couldn't take the chance that Daughtery, for whatever reason, might leave the stage at any stop. Stopping at each of the stations would consume time, but he had to be sure that the rancher remained on the stage.

They stopped at two more relay stations before dusk. Then, as the moon lit the sky behind the mountain peaks, but dark shadows still bathed the forest floor, Slade reined up at a bend in the road. Ahead, yellow squares of light marked the next relay station. Cautiously, they rode ahead, Slade's hand near his .44.

Nana remained in the shadows as the young half-breed rode up to the hitching rail and hallooed the station. The door swung open and a rectangle of light spilled out on the ground. A bowlegged man with a battered Spencer peered into the darkness.

"Howdy," said Slade, holding his hands out to his side. "Saw your light and hoped you might have run across a friend of mine."

The bowlegged man studied Slade and his horse. "Who's out there with you?"

"Just me, partner."

The old man considered Slade's answer, then nodded. "Come on in if you be hungry. Grub's hot, and the straw's soft out to the barn. Who's this hombre you're lookin' for?"

The mention of grub caused Slade's stomach to knot with hunger, but he remembered Nana. The Apache was just as hungry as Slade. Later, they would eat. He described John Daughtery.

The bowlegged man nodded. "Yep. He was here."

"Was?"

"Rode in with the stage, then bought a broomtail roan and headed on down the road. Something about some kind of accident in Santa Fe he had to get to and couldn't wait for the stage."

Slade shook his head. "Reckon that's him. Appreciate the offer of grub, but I dearly need to find this friend of mine."

Back in the shadows, Nana and Slade discussed whether to ride after dark and take a chance that Daughtery was indeed heading for Santa Fe, or to bed down

237

nearby and take up the trail in the morning just in case the rancher decided to cut off the road.

They decided to take the chance that he would not leave the road. They rode until midnight before pulling into a shallow glen and bedding down for the night. Despite the ache in his empty stomach, Slade fell asleep as soon as his head touched the sod.

Succulent aromas invaded his restless dreams. Slade awakened before sunrise to see Nana squatting by a small fire roasting two rabbits to a golden brown perfection.

When Nana saw that Slade was awake, he gestured to the rabbits. "Eat."

The young half-breed wasted no time. After he finished the rabbit, he drank from a nearby stream. He rose, patted his stomach, and said, "After a feast like that, I'm ready to take on anything."

An hour later, they reached the next relay station.

Slade returned at a gallop. Daughtery had not shown up. That meant that he was somewhere behind them. As they had feared, he had pulled off the road, and they had ridden right past his trail.

Ten miles down the road, Slade found tracks leading off the road into the forest.

"Are you certain it is the one we seek?"

Slade nodded to the road. There was only one set of tracks other than those left by the stage. "Nope. But they're fresh — within the last ten-twelve hours. What do you figure the odds are on two yahoos cutting off the same road on the same night?"

Nana shrugged and fell in behind Slade, but Nana's question nagged at the young half-breed. What if they were tracking the wrong man? John Daughtery could use the precious extra time to hide his trail so deep in the forest that not even a whole tribe of Apaches could find him.

The faint trail led over a sawtooth ridge and down into a valley. Slade pulled into a young stand of conifers when he saw that the trail intersected a second trail ahead, one worn from use. In the distance, a thin column of smoke drifted up through the pines on the side of a ridge. Between them and the ridge was a mile-wide meadow forming a semicircle around the smoke. The location was, Slade noted, an ideal spot for a hideout.

Without a word, the two men headed deeper into the forest as they began a wide swing around the smoke. Thirty minutes later, they looked down on a small cabin from a narrow ledge that descended to the rawhide and greenstick corral behind the cabin. A single horse, a long-haired roan, stood hipshot in the middle of the corral, its head drooping.

Dismounting, Slade gestured to one side of the cabin. "I'll cover the other side."

Suddenly, a rifle cracked and a slug ricocheted off a nearby boulder. Slade pulled his .44 and threw a hasty shot toward the cabin. In the next instant, an ear-splitting explosion ripped the mountain air, its concussion rocking Slade back on his heels. Immediately, a yellowish orange cloud billowed into the air where the cabin had been.

CHAPTER TWENTY

"Duck," yelled Slade, throwing himself to the ground at the base of a pine as debris from the cabin rained down on them.

When the smoke cleared, nothing remained of the cabin except smoldering splinters of wood. Slade cursed as he studied the devastation. "What do you reckon he was doing with that much black powder?"

"Who can say," Nana replied. "The white man's ways are strange to me."

Slade glanced at his Apache brother who wore a faint grin. He shook his head and turned back to study the ruins of the cabin. Fifty feet away, he found the cantle and part of the fender of a fancy saddle inlaid with silver, the leather singed by the fire and the inlays scratched and scarred. He looked around, his eyes searching the area for the remains of the saddle as well as burning paper. There was none.

"For what do you look?" asked Nana.

Slade frowned. "Money. Daughtery had a wad of bills. After an explosion like this, there should be some around, unless he buried it. And I don't think he was the burying kind."

Nana grasped Slade's implication. "You do not believe this was Daughtery?"

"No. Daughtery's been here and gone. There's a roan in the corral, the one he bought at the relay station." He nodded to the remnants of the saddle. "Look at that fancy rig. I don't figure anyone at the station had a saddle like this to sell. It must have belonged to that unlucky jasper in the cabin." He gestured to the debris. "You see another saddle around anywhere?"

"What if this one we follow is not Daughtery?"

Slade looked around at Nana, reading the unspoken doubt in his brother's eyes. With a determined set to his jaw, Slade said, "The one we follow is Daughtery."

"Maybe. If he is not, we have lost much time."

"The time is not wasted." The young half-breed nodded to the mountains spreading to the west. "Daughtery's out there. I figure he rode in, swapped horses with whoever this jasper was, and told him we were following. Maybe he made us out to be lawmen. That would explain why this old boy pulled down on us without a word." He paused and looked around. To the east, a sawtooth ridge with a saddle marked the horizon. "If I was in Daughtery's shoes, I'd head that way. I'd forget about Santa Fe and hope whoever was chasing me wouldn't."

Nana grinned. His brother had lost none of his craftiness during his time with the white man. "Let us see." The Apache brave had no doubt Slade could cling to their quarry's trail. His only question was to the identity of their prey.

By evening, Slade and Nana had cut sign. The man they trailed had moved out north of the cabin, but within half a mile, he began a looping swing to the east.

They made camp early.

John Daughtery must have heard the explosion, Slade told himself, second-guessing the rustler. He figured that Daughtery would suppose that either his pursuers were killed, or they believed Daughtery himself was killed in the explosion. Slade decided that the rustler would relax now that he believed he had suckered them, but Slade was not going to relax.

After a satisfying meal of baked trout, they extinguished the fire, rode a mile off the trail, and bedded down in a young stand of pine. Both men fell into a sound sleep.

They awakened only when a light gray sky forecast the dawn. Nana brewed tea, and they finished the trout from the night before. After the sun rose, they moved back to the trail.

Before the sun burned the dew from the grass, they had lost the trail again.

"Where in the hell did he go now?" Slade exclaimed, backtracking down the icy stream they had followed for the last thirty minutes.

"There," said Nana, pointing to an overturned stone beneath a broken pine branch. Slade stared down at the stone, studying the scar on the mossy underbelly. Leaning from his saddle, he picked up the stone and ran a finger over the scar, a white streak of powder across the stone. Fresh.

Ahead of them, a rock-littered slope curved out of the stream into a stand of young spruce, scant years from the burn that had destroyed the previous stand of giant Engelmanns. The tracks on the slope were almost invisible, a scarred rock here, one overturned farther along. Slade shook his head. Daughtery might not be much on picking horseflesh, but he was a damn sight smarter about hiding his trail.

Slade pursed his lips. He had been wrong last night when he guessed Daughtery would relax his guard — if this was really John Daughtery, Slade reminded himself, remembering Nana's concern. He admitted to himself that the possibility was very real that Daughtery might have been blown to pieces back in the cabin and that they could be tracking a stranger.

But he couldn't convince himself they were pursuing a stranger. Otherwise, why would their prey try to cover his trail so carefully? Still, once Slade glimpsed his quarry, he would feel better.

The trail led up the slope, doubled back to the stream below, then angled upward over a humpback ridge two miles distant.

"He don't ride like anyone in a big hurry to get somewhere," Slade remarked.

Nana grunted and pointed out where the rider had doubled back once again.

Tracking was slow, but their quarry was not making much better time than they, Slade reminded himself when he felt his frustration building over their slow progress.

Just before dark, Slade caught a glimpse of their prey in a grassy meadow far below. The light was too poor and the distance too great to discern the features of the man. They waited until the rider disappeared into the forest.

"I'd say we bed down right here," Slade said. "He won't ride much farther tonight. Maybe we'll get lucky and spot his fire from up here." But deep inside, Slade knew the man below was too smart to build a fire.

As they dismounted, the rider far below stood just inside the wall of lodgepole pines along the edge of the meadow and stared back up the mountain. A grin spread across John Daughtery's face.

Slade and the Apache were in his backyard now.

After he had fled from the law back East several years earlier, this was the region where he hid out for two years, during which time he had become as familiar with this part of New Mexico Territory as he was with the beard on his face. With a chuckle, he headed deeper into the forest.

He had plans for them if they hung to his trail.

The next morning, Slade and Nana moved out early. Half a mile into the forest, the young half-breed pulled up. He looked at Nana, wondering if his brother was as puzzled as he. "You see what I see?"

"Yes. The man makes no effort to hide his tracks."

"It's like he wants us to follow him."

The two studied the sign. The trail led over fresh soil instead of rocky plate, through grassy clearings rather than leaf-filled basins, along the soft edge of tiny streams instead of in the middle of the rocky beds.

The back of Slade's neck prickled as the trail twisted through giant boulders, all the time steadily ascending the mountain. The trail led alongside a looming wall of granite fifty feet high. After a quarter of a mile, the trail cut into the granite wall, a trail so narrow he could touch the walls on either side of the rocky path. There was little room to turn around.

He glanced back at Nana, who nodded. If Slade had ever seen a perfect spot for an ambush, this was it. He halted. Ahead, a granite ledge extended over the trail, creating a low tunnel forty feet long through solid granite. They would have to duck to pass under it.

"I don't like it," Slade said over his shoulder.

Nana's black eyes narrowed and his broad nostrils flared as he picked up the musty odor emanating from the darkness of the tunnel. "Back. Move back," Nana growled, pulling on the reins and forcing his horse to stutter step backward.

Before Slade could move, an explosion erupted at the far end of the tunnel. Black smoke and tongues of fire belched out of the mouth of the tunnel. Within seconds, half a dozen rattlesnakes slithered from the cave, some thick as a human thigh.

The rumble of shifting boulders sounded over Slade's head.

Frightened, his horse whinnied and reared, trying to turn around. The trail was too narrow. The horse pawed at the rocky wall. A hoof caught in a narrow crack. The buckskin jerked, but its hoof had wedged tight in the cleft. Its eyes rolling with fear, the animal lunged forward, then threw itself back. For a moment, Slade was pinned against the wall, but he managed to throw himself free just as the frightened animal lost its balance. Its leg snapped sharply like the crack of a Winchester, and the horse fell to the ground, jammed between the narrow walls.

The young half-breed bounced off the granite wall and slammed to the ground. The back of his head cracked against the granite. Flashing white stars exploded in his head, and his muscles went limp. He lay there, stunned, struggling to retain his consciousness

The razor-sharp sound of splitting granite

cut through the fog swirling through his head. The ground shook as a great boulder slammed to the ground behind him.

The frightened squeal of his buckskin pushed back the darkness threatening to engulf him. He lurched to his feet, and, extending one hand to brace himself against the wall, staggered down the narrow trail after Nana. His head ached, and his shoulder throbbed.

Abruptly, he stumbled up against a vertical wall. Shaking his head to clear his blurred vision, Slade saw that the explosion had fractured a ledge of granite, part of which had plunged down to wedge between the granite walls like a third wall, blocking his retreat.

He jerked around as the buckskin whinnied frantically. Eyes wide with terror, the animal tried vainly to struggle to its feet as the first rattlesnake struck. Another struck, and then another, injecting massive doses of poison into the squealing animal. Without hesitation, Slade pulled his .44 and shot the agonizing animal between the eyes.

He took a step back and fired again, this time blowing the head off a rattler. But another and then another slithered from the cave, driven by the explosion. Slade didn't bother to count the number, but one was too many, and right now, a heap more than one was heading in his direction.

He fired twice more. The slugs hurled two rattlesnakes into those behind, causing the oncoming rattlers to strike at the limp bodies of their own kind.

Holstering his revolver, Slade quickly scanned the vertical walls surrounding him. They were thirty feet high, and the nearest handhold was a narrow fissure in the granite fifteen feet above the trail.

The rattlers drew closer, a mottled brown blanket of death. The only chance Slade had was to walk his way up the wall by pressing his back and hands against one side of the narrow trail and his feet against the other. With luck, he could ease his way up the fissure. A slim chance, but — he looked at the rattlers. He had no choice.

Pressing his hands against the granite, he jammed his back against the wall and reached out with his foot, trying to dig his toes into the granite. The rattlesnakes drew closer. Keeping his upper body slightly above his feet, Slade began inching up the wall, step by step.

By the time he was five feet above the trail, the rattlesnakes had reached the granite wedge that blocked the trail. Several coiled and struck out at those in the rear. His shoulders ached. His fingers throbbed. Sweat poured down Slade's back, soaking his linen shirt and stinging his eyes. A toe slipped, but he caught himself before plunging down into the mass of serpents.

Their rattles hummed, a chattering cacophony that infused a fierce spirit into his determination. Flexing his toes through his moccasins to grasp at the granite wall, the young half-breed wished he'd had the foresight to remove the moccasins. Bare feet would have provided a surer grip.

He wormed one foot up, then supporting his torso with his hands, the opposite shoulder. His fingers clawed into the wall below him. Slowly, painfully, he inched up the wall. Halfway up to the top, the muscles in his legs began to spasm. His toes cramped. For several seconds, he remained motionless, gathering his strength. He felt a foot slip, not much, but enough to tell him that his strength was failing rapidly.

He threw a hasty glance at the ground beneath him. If he fell, he would be dead within seconds. He tried to scoot his back up the wall, but the muscles in his legs had lost their strength. He sucked in a deep breath for one last mighty effort.

CHAPTER TWENTY-ONE

Suddenly, a rawhide lariat fell across his chest. "Hold on."

Slade recognized Nana's voice and grabbed for the lariat. Seconds later, his legs trembling from the strain, he stood beside Nana, looking down on the nest of serpents. Without a word, Nana climbed down the ledge and backtracked down the trail. Slade followed.

"What now?" The Apache studied the mouth of the trail, halfway expecting to see the rattlers appearing at any moment.

Slade glanced at the mountain towering over them. Its walls were sheer and smooth, offering no sign of a route over them. He nodded to the valley below. "Drop down there and then swing around this ridge. Cut his sign on the other side of the tunnel where he set off the black powder or dynamite."

Nana gestured for Slade to mount the

gray. The young half-breed refused. Nana insisted. "You still weak. You ride. Later I ride," said the Apache brave, turning his back and heading back down the trail to the valley on foot.

Two hours later, they studied the trail from the other side of the ridge. A narrow black line snaked over the trail. Residue from the black powder used to set off the explosion that had driven the serpents from their dens.

Farther up the trail, they found an empty powder keg. "He must have a place around here," noted Slade, studying the mountain above them.

The trap increased Slade's respect for John Daughtery. He had never questioned the man's bravery or determination, but now he realized that the rustler was also immeasurably devious, capable of plotting the unexpected, very much like the Apache. Each step from here on out would have to be guarded.

At a trot, Nana led the way. The trail twisted like a snake as it ascended the mountain in a series of cutbacks. Finally it topped out on a narrow bench, against the back of which sat a weathered cabin. Spinning on his heel, Nana grabbed the lark's head bridle and backed the horse down the trail out of sight of the cabin as Slade slid from the animal's back.

The two of them dropped into a crouch and eased back up the trail so they could peer over the rim of the bench and study the cabin. The front door gaped open at a skewed angle with one hinge broken. The back of the windowless cabin was spang up against the vertical wall of the mountain.

Slade elbowed Nana and nodded to the moist horse biscuits a few feet from them. Daughtery, or someone, had been here. But where was the horse? The bench was less than a quarter mile in length, completely devoid of vegetation, bare as if it had been freshly broom swept. There were no corrals, no barns, no indication of any means to contain an animal. Slade doubted that the corral would be down below the bench. Mountain lions relished horse meat. Any jasper with sense corralled his animals where he could keep an eye on them.

That could mean only one thing.

"There's a cave behind the cabin," he whispered to Nana, who nodded without speaking. "You wait here. I'll slip around to the other side of the ledge. We'll get him between us. When I signal, we'll move in."

A wry grin broke across Nana's face. "We will have much protection," he said with

254

irony, nodding to the barren plateau.

Slade shrugged. "You could always outrun me."

"Then let us ask the Sun and Moon not to make it necessary once again."

"I already have," whispered Slade as he departed.

A few minutes later, he gave the call of the whippoorwill. Rising into a crouch, he eased toward the silent cabin, his muscles bunched, his balance on the balls of his feet, his .44 clutched in his hand. On the far side of the bench, Nana appeared in a similar posture.

Overhead the sun baked down, hot and dry as only the sun can be on an autumn day in the mountains. Birds sang. A squirrel chattered.

Sweat ran down Slade's forehead, stinging his eyes. Tension knotted his stomach. He flexed his fingers on the butt of his .44, noting how slick this made the grip of the Colt.

Step after step, he moved closer, eyes fastened on the darkness behind the door, wondering if a Winchester were in there, trained on him. Halfway across the clearing, he began to relax. Had Daughtery been in the cabin, he would not have allowed the two men to draw so close. Now, by the time he fired once, then swung his gun around, the other man would be out of sight by the side of the house.

The cabin was deserted. In the middle of the room sat a table constructed of split logs. A black wood stove backed up to one wall. Against the opposite wall, empty dynamite boxes littered the floor. The fourth wall was a canvas drape behind which, as Slade expected, was a yawning cave.

Carrying a torch of lighter pine, Slade stepped into the cave. The smell of turpentine from the torch burned his nostrils. Nana squatted by him and pointed to a set of horse tracks in the dust. "He come this way."

Slade studied the ground. "I don't see that he came out either."

Nana shook his head as he rose and stared into Slade's eyes. "He is in the cave."

With a nod, Slade said, "Then we'll go in after him." The idea did not appeal to the young half-breed, not after the trap Daughtery had laid for them with the rattlesnakes. He swallowed the copper taste of fear in his mouth and looked at Nana. Fear was in his brother's eyes also.

Leading the gray, the two men headed deeper into the damp cave, their torches punching dim holes in the suffocating blackness. The tunnel forked a hundred yards into the cave, the larger of the two angling to the east while the smaller cut sharply to the north.

Slade knelt and studied the floor of the cave. The tracks of the horse were clearly discernible in the damp soil, their edges nice and sharp. A sheen of water lay over the bottom of the track. Slade frowned. Something seemed out of place, not quite in tune. "He isn't far ahead, but —" Slade ran his finger around the sharp perimeter of the horse print. "But he's moving slow — too slow — that way." He nodded to the east. Almost like he wanted to be sure they did not lose him, Slade thought to himself.

A wry grin spread over Nana's face. Slade recognized it as reluctant admiration for John Daughtery's cunning. "Cave has another opening," Nana said.

Slade shook his head, Nana's observation making him discard his last thought. "It figures."

He jerked to a halt and sniffed the air. The sharp, bitter smell of burning black powder stung his nostrils. Damn! How could he have been so stupid? He had been right. Daughtery had wanted them to follow. He spun back to Nana. "Quick —"

An explosion rocked the cave, knocking Slade to the ground. He curled his arms over his head against falling rocks. The entire mountain rumbled and groaned. Slowly, the groans died away, punctuated by the sharp crack of splitting granite. He opened his eyes. The torches burned weakly where they lay on the damp floor. Dust thicker than the North Carolina sea fog in which Slade had fought during the War of Secession filled the cave, clogging his nostrils, choking his throat. Nana called his name.

"Over here," he coughed. A torch lay within arm's reach, emitting a weak flame and a thin stream of black smoke. Pushing himself to his feet, he reached for the torch, aware that Nana had moved up beside him. "I should have guessed what Daughtery was up to," Slade muttered, searching vainly for his hat and the other torch. "Especially when I saw the empty dynamite boxes back in the cabin."

Nana grunted, "Now we must find way out."

With the aid of the torch, which was less than twelve inches in length now, they felt their way through the dust only to discover that both ends of the cave were sealed by great boulders. There was no sign of the horse.

"He must be under there," said Nana,

nodding to the boulders blocking their way.

Slade eyed the jumble of boulders warily, wondering if the explosions had disturbed any rattlesnake dens. For several moments, he remained motionless, staring at the boulders. Suddenly, the torch flickered, the tip of its flame darting toward him.

Both men knew instinctively what the darting flame meant. Extending the torch to arm's length, Slade traced the torch around the granite walls, searching for another random gust of fresh air. As he turned back to the middle of the cave, the flame brightened. They followed the dancing flame toward the far end of the cave, but as they passed the narrow tunnel leading to the north, the flame leaped behind them.

"In there," whispered Slade, holding the torch into the small tunnel. Less than five feet high, the tunnel was as round as the shaft of any arrow Slade had ever crafted. The cave angled steeply upward for several yards before dropping away from their sight.

Without hesitation, Slade led the way up the tunnel. Each man knew this was his only choice. Digging out through the tumble of rocks and boulders was impossible. The narrow tunnel was their only chance — a slim one, but a chance.

The floor of the tunnel sloped away into darkness, the same direction the flickering flames from the diminishing torch leaped. The opening to which the air moved was somewhere ahead. The black smoke from the torch burned his eyes, and the stench of burning resin stung his nostrils. At the foot of the slope, the tunnel curved to the left.

Slade attempted to maintain his bearings as the narrow tunnel twisted and curved. Each time the tunnel forked, he followed the one that fed his torch. Abruptly the contour of the cave changed from round to an oval shape, the top crushing down to meet the bottom. The lighter pine torch was only inches long now.

Dropping to his hands and knees, Slade inched forward, all the while his eyes searching the tunnel for rattlesnakes. His chest ached, and he realized he had been holding his breath. He forced himself to breathe slowly, regularly.

Slade froze as the tiny flame brightened. He felt the chill of air against the sweat on the back of his neck. Ahead, the floor sloped down into a dark pool of water. He squeezed his eyes shut. Close places had never bothered him, but now —

He squinted his eyes into the flickering shadows. The water came within a foot of the top of the tunnel. He held the torch out. The flame licked greedily toward the water, eating away at the lighter pine torch.

He heard Nana's harsh breathing behind him. He looked over his shoulder. "Ready?"

The stoic calm the Apache always wore crumbled. "No," he replied simply. "Not ready."

Slade forced a weak chuckle. "We got no choice."

Nana drew a deep breath and closed his eyes. After several seconds, he opened them and nodded. "I follow."

Slade looked around and jerked back. A black water snake glided across the surface toward them. Suddenly, the snake spied them and doubled back on itself, its sinuous body shooting through the water in fear.

Slade swallowed the lump in his throat. Damn. How many more snakes were in the water? As a boy in the mountains and later with the Apache, he possessed no fear of snakes, but he respected them. Though the snakes usually tried to escape, more than once he had been witness to accidental encounters where both the serpent and the man reached the same spot at the same time. He hoped that didn't happen now, in a dark cave, underwater, and with a torch about to burn itself out.

"Let's go," he muttered, forced to crawl on his knees through the water and try to keep the flame burning hoping to frighten off any other snakes. Slade had heard the theory that snakes did not strike under water, but he, for one, was not anxious to put it to a test.

The water was like ice. A spring. That's what they had discovered, a spring. His hopes soared. With luck, an opening was nearby.

Slade half crawled, half sat, scooting through the water that was now up to his neck, wondering what the snake had been doing in such cold water. He glanced at the roof of the cave, his eyes searching for any fissures through which the snake might have fallen. He saw nothing.

The tunnel curved. But around the bend, only more darkness greeted them. Slade's body was growing numb. By now, he was holding only a splinter of pine from which a tiny but bright flame struggled to push back the darkness.

"Soon we'll have to go on in the dark," he said over his shoulder. Despite the icy water, perspiration beaded on his forehead and stung his eyes.

Nana grunted.

Abruptly Slade halted. The water was up

to his chin now. He extended the tiny torch and caught his breath when he saw the top of the cave slope to less than an inch above the surface of the water. "Looks like this is as far as we go," he muttered.

"Then we swim under the water," Nana said from the darkness behind Slade.

A cold hand squeezed his heart. At first, he had considered backtracking out of the tunnel, but Nana was right. They must go on. With Apache fatalism, he accepted the belief that if this was his time, there was nothing he could do about it. Suddenly, the torch burned his fingers. He dropped the splinter and darkness engulfed them.

"Look," exclaimed Slade, his excited voice a hollow echo in the cave. "There's light ahead."

Sure enough, a dull glow shone through the water.

"I'll go first. Give me a few seconds, then follow," he said.

"I will wait."

Taking a deep breath, Slade slipped under the water and swam toward the glow. With each stroke, the light grew brighter. Thirty seconds later, he broke the surface of a small pool of spring water nestled between two grassy knolls.

He climbed out of the water and drew in

a deep breath of fresh air, reveling in the bright sunshine warming his body. Moments later, Nana broke the surface and swam ashore. They grinned at each other, and each understood the other's unspoken relief.

While Slade reconnoitered, trying to discover their location before the sun set, Nana set about rummaging up some grub. When Slade returned after dark, the Apache had a small fire blazing brightly in the nook formed by two out thrusts of granite. Two trout sizzled on a spit cradled between two forked branches stuck in the ground.

The young half-breed nodded across the mountain. "The cabin's two miles east of us and about a half mile above."

"The cave doubled back then."

Slade nodded. "And then some." He pinched some flaky white flesh from a trout. Juggling the hot meat in his hands, he blew on it gently. "Tomorrow, we'll cross the mountain and pick up Daughtery's sign."

Nana eyed him for several seconds. "What if this man is not Daughtery?"

Slade had been worrying about that very possibility more than he wanted to admit. After all this time without seeing their prey except for one fleeting glimpse, the young half-breed had the feeling they had been chasing a ghost. But even if their quarry were a ghost, Slade and Nana were closing in. An angry glint sparked in Slade's gray eyes. "I don't care who he is, Daughtery or not. It's payback time for this jasper."

The dark Apache grinned and reached for his own trout. This was an anger he understood, a vengeance he approved.

CHAPTER TWENTY-TWO

Early next morning, they broke camp. By noon they located the cave exit on the opposite side of the mountain and cut their quarry's sign. "We haven't seen this cowpoke up close, but I'd bet the ranch that it's John Daughtery."

"He is a wise man," said Nana, looking down the trail where it disappeared among the pines. "He knows much of the mountains and its animals."

"Wise?" Slade snorted. "I don't know if I'd go that far."

Nana looked back at his brother with a look of pained tolerance. "Wisdom is that which you learn by experience. All of us, even an evil man, can learn."

A sheepish grin came to Slade's lips. "One thing's for damned sure, he knows this place like a second home," he said, gesturing to the towering peaks and forests around them. Slade paused and looked at Nana. When he spoke, concern filled his voice. "If this isn't Daughtery, I just hope I haven't wasted whatever time Bent has."

Nana looked deep into his brother's eyes. "We have done our best. No more can be asked."

Slade hung on to their quarry's sign with the tenacity of a badger digging a rabbit out of its den. The trail zigzagged, doubled back, then crisscrossed rocky slopes, through brush-choked coulees, and up boulder-strewn streams, but all the time in a general sweep back to the west.

"To Santa Fe," Slade announced, looking up from where he was kneeling and inspecting the sign. "He's still heading for Santa Fe."

"Through the country of the Ute," Nana said, an ominous warning in his tone.

Later in the day, the trail straightened. Their quarry had decided to make a run for it.

That night, Slade stood on a rounded out thrust overlooking a sprawling valley of pine and aspen far below. The valley merged darkly into the horizon miles to the west. He searched the silent panorama before him, hoping to spot a flicker of firelight, a spot of yellow in the darkness, any sign that their man was within striking distance.

He saw nothing. Nor had he expected to. Daughtery was too smart not to hide his fire, especially in Ute country.

In the distance, a coyote wailed. Behind him, an owl hooted, and down below, a rabbit shrieked.

"Maybe our luck will be better in the morning," he muttered, climbing into his bedroll.

Nana grunted. "Snow comes with the morning."

Slade cursed. "So much for luck."

The morning sky was gray with snow clouds. As Nana had predicted, soft flakes began falling as the false dawn pushed the darkness to the west. Slade shivered over the small fire. Wild raspberry tea steamed around the hot rocks dropped in a bowl fashioned from bark. Rabbits browned on spits. Slade shook his head as he tightened his belt a notch. "My stomach's gnawing at my backbone. I reckon I could sure put myself around a slab of fat beef."

Nana grinned, the creases in his cheeks indicating his loss of weight also. "At least we have the rabbit."

Squatting, Slade used a crudely fashioned wooden spoon to sip the tea. "Well, the good Lord would've made it a lot easier for us if He'd been obliged to stick some fat on these rabbits."

"We need horses," said Nana before tearing off a chunk of meat with his even white teeth. "Now that the trail runs straight, we must ride hard to catch him before the snow covers his tracks."

To the north, thicker clouds pushed over the mountain peaks. Slade grimaced. There was bad weather ahead. "I still say he's bound for Santa Fe."

The clouds grew thicker throughout the morning, but the snowfall remained light. Nana led the way at a steady mile-eating trot, his keen eyes picking up sign.

Just before noon, Nana pulled up. Slade stopped by his side, neither man breathing hard, for the rigorous twenty-mile runs as Apache youth had hardened their muscles and strengthened their lungs. Sladed studied the new sign in the snow that the Apache brave was inspecting.

Nana looked up. "Four, maybe five horses." His eyes narrowed. "Utes."

The wiry half-breed set his jaw as his gaze followed the tracks back to a thick stand of aspens from which the Utes had come. This man, Daughtery or not, was his. Damned be any man, Ute or otherwise, that tried to take the rustler away from him. "Looks like five to me. You sure they're Utes?"

Nana knelt again and traced his forefinger around the perimeter of an unshod track. "We are in their country. The Ute are cowards, but five of them against one white man makes them brave."

"If it is Ute, that means they go against Ouray."

The squatting Apache grunted. A cynical grin curled his lips. "Many Utes are against Chief Ouray. A brother from the White Mountain Apache has said that the Ute chief has considered selling much Ute tribal land to the bluecoats."

"That will bring trouble."

Nana stood up. "For Ouray and the soldiers."

Slade studied the sign at Nana's feet. A deer had stepped in the middle of one of the tracks. A few feet beyond, at the edge of a pristine brook, the tiny prints of a raccoon also crossed the trail. "They probably stumbled across his sign this morning," he said, noting the snow had not yet filled the Ute tracks. "I hope to hell he keeps his eyes open," Slade added, a sinking feeling in the pit of his stomach. Five to one was bad enough odds, and if they surprised him — Slade shook his head. The man would have no chance at all.

The snow grew heavier, falling in fat flakes that clung to their shoulders, fat flakes that quickly covered the trail.

They pushed on, moving fast to catch their quarry, but at the same time their keen eyes probing and studying every shadow that danced through the forest. Among the aspen and pine, the trail was easy to follow, but in the meadows, snow covered the sign, forcing them to cast about for the trail.

At noon, they cut the trail on the edge of a meadow.

Midafternoon, Slade caught the unmistakably bitter smell of burning pine. The stinging, astringent odor of turpentine cut through the clean and crisp freshness of new snow. "Utes."

Nana nodded. His pan-shaped face was hard, his black eyes cold. Slade cursed his luck as he glided through the forest.

The two men angled up the mountain, wanting to look down on the camp. Like wraiths, Slade and Nana floated through the forest from shadow to shadow, over rocky ledges, along snow-drifted coulees until they reached an upthrust of granite at the head of a small meadow.

Slade's blood ran cold as he focused his eyes on the scene at the opposite end of the meadow, almost a quarter of a mile distant. It was not the Utes that chilled him, but the naked white man strung off the ground between two pines. A rope was tied around each wrist and fastened around limbs high in the pines. Ropes were tied around each ankle and then staked to the ground, spreading his body in the shape of an X.

Brandishing knives, two of the Utes danced around the man, pausing occasionally to lunge at the white man and slash at his flesh. The other three Utes sat on the ground before a fire, passing a bottle between them.

Slade looked for a beard, to make sure it was John Daughtery he had been pursuing, but the man's back was to Slade, and his head was slumped forward on his chest. Even at this distance, Slade could see how the Utes had savagely tortured the man. From shoulder to heel, wide strips of skin had been peeled from his back and legs, leaving a gory pattern of red and white stripes from shoulder to heel.

Torture outraged Slade even though he knew well that to some tribes, torture was a means of displaying their respect for a brave man. But the majority of the tribes tortured for the same reason the Utes now tortured the white man, out of cruelty and self-gratification.

The grass in the meadow was belly high. The snow bent the crowns of the grass in a gentle arc. Slade touched Nana's arm and glanced across the meadow. The Apache brave understood. With only handguns, they had to get closer. Silently, they slipped down into the meadow and slithered through the thick grass.

The Utes were too engrossed in their games of drinking and torture to notice the grass moving against the wind. Ahead of Slade, a rabbit burst out of hiding and dashed across the meadow, but the Utes ignored it.

By now, Nana and Slade had covered half the distance to the camp. The snowfall grew heavier. Cold flakes stung the back of Slade's neck. Slade whispered, "That's it, fellers. You just keep paying no attention to what's going on around you. And tonight, you powwow with your granddaddies."

The drunken laughter continued. The closer to the camp, the louder the laughter. Slade peered over the grass. He was within thirty yards of the camp, close enough to hear the moans of the dying white man. He glanced at Nana and drew his .44 before easing forward again.

Though he was the best shot in his tribe

and a skilled marksman in the War of Secession, Slade preferred shorter distances, for handguns were notoriously inaccurate.

He paused. He raised his head. When he did, he was staring in the eyes of a surprised Ute not more than twenty feet away.

Slade leaped to his feet, his gun roaring. From the corner of his eye, he saw Nana dashing to the right, toward the horses, his six-gun blazing.

The first slug caught the surprised Ute between the eyes, and the back of his skull exploded, spraying blood and brains over the startled Indians behind. Two broke for their horses only to find Nana waiting for them. Neither had time to reach his saddle gun.

The meadow echoed with the boom of gunfire, and the echoes rolled down the mountain.

Slade's next two slugs punched side-by-side holes in the fourth Ute and sent him spinning to the ground. The last Indian broke into the forest. Two 180 grains of lead severed his spine, sending him sprawling headlong, dead before he finished sliding through the snow on his belly.

Before taking another step, Slade quickly reloaded. Cautiously, he checked the Indians. Satisfied that they were dead, he holstered his revolver and turned to the white man. It was John Daughtery, his once white beard now rust colored by his own blood.

But Slade felt no relief, only outrage. He closed his eyes and shook his head when he saw the savagery executed on the rustler. The ropes around his wrists had cut off all circulation. His hands were black, dead. His eyes had been gouged from their sockets. One dangled on his cheek, rolling obscenely from nose to cheekbone in the wind. The other lay squashed in the snow and mud. To complete the job, the Utes had castrated him.

Daughtery moaned. Quickly Slade and Nana cut his bonds and gently lowered him to the ground, but each movement brought screams of pain from his bloody lips.

"Daughtery. It's me, Slade," the young half-breed whispered. "Can you hear me?"

The old man's head rolled from side to side. His throat worked, trying to force words from his lips.

Slade leaned forward. "What is it?"

His voice was a scratchy rasp. "Pl-please, kill me. Kill me."

Slade glanced up at Nana, who watched impassively. The Apache shook his head and nodded at the blood-soaked ground over which Daughtery had been tied. It was a wonder the old man was not already dead.

He touched Daughtery's shoulder. "Listen to me. You remember Bledsoe, Wiley Bledsoe?" No response. Slade asked. "Who killed Wiley Bledsoe?"

"H-hurt. I hurt."

"Wiley Bledsoe. Who killed him?"

A sneer curled one side of Daughtery's cracked lips. Bright crimson blood appeared in one of the cracks. With one last effort, he spat blood at Slade, and then a deep rasp came from his chest. His body shuddered, stiffened, and then his lips went slack.

His cold eyes remaining on John Daughtery, Slade shook his head. "Bastard," he muttered. Still glaring at the dead man, he said, "We've done a heap of riding for nothing."

Nana had been searching through Daughtery's belongings. He held up a money belt. "This will help."

Slade snapped open one pocket and thumbed through the tightly packed bills. "It still won't tell us who killed Wiley Bledsoe, and I'd rather have that answer than ten times this much money," he said, closing the pocket and fastening the belt around his waist.

"Who can say?" A trace of cynicism edged Nana's words. "Money means much to the white man. And the Mormon is a white man."

With a shrug, Slade reached for his knife. The ground was still soft. A grave would not take long to dig. Suddenly, he felt a vibration through the soles of his moccasins. He looked down the valley. Nothing. He glanced around at Nana, who was already racing for the horses.

CHAPTER
TWENTY-THREE

Utes!

Without hesitation, Slade grabbed the rawhide reins and swung aboard a thick-muscled Indian pony with wide haunches. He dug his heels into the pony's flank and the animal leaped forward.

Nana, astride a long-haired roan, pulled up beside Slade, a grin on his face. Slade knew the meaning of the smile. No Apache likes to run. He prefers to stand and fight, even against overwhelming odds. Nana was telling Slade that was what they should do. Stand and fight.

With the snow stinging his face, Slade shook his head and leaned over the pony's neck. Bent came first.

They deliberately raced along the edge of the meadow within scant feet of the forest not only to break their silhouette but to provide a fast means of disappearance should the Utes begin firing at them.

From behind, a chorus of yells echoed across the valley. Slade threw a look over his shoulder. A dozen screaming Utes broke out of the forest at the far end of the meadow. The sound of rifle fire popped. Slugs ripped through the nearby trees.

The forest made a sweeping curve to their left before cutting sharply back to the right. Slade followed the curve, then whipped around the cutback, leaning over the pony's withers. Beyond the cutback, Slade angled away from the meadow and up a slope of burned timber. Giant pines sprawled over the landscape like toothpicks strewn across a table. Their blackened limbs, naked of needles, but with crowns of snow, punctured the sky like the spines of some giant porcupine.

Another series of shots rang out, peppering the trees behind them and kicking up the snow at their horse's feet. He glanced over his shoulder. Nana's grin broadened.

Slade shifted his weight, aiding the small pony as it twisted its way through the fallen trees. He topped the slope. Below, charred trees covered the steep slope, their burned limbs probing the sky. The vague outline of the trail descended through the burn to the base of the mountain and curled into a stand of green pines. Once they reached the pines below, they were safe.

Halfway down the hill, Slade heard a yell from above. The popping of rifle fire echoed down the slope. Slugs tore up the ground ahead of his running pony. The animal stumbled, then caught itself as the mountainside fell away.

The next instant seared itself in Slade's brain. He heard the distinctive snap of the horse's leg from behind, followed by the frightened squeal of a pony and the scraping sound of a heavy body sliding in the mud and snow. There came a brief silence, then something that sounded like a fist slamming against a door, and then a grunt.

He glanced over his shoulder. His blood chilled.

Impaled through the chest, Nana hung limply on a blackened limb where he had been hurled when his pony snapped its leg and stumbled. The frightened animal squealed, but Slade heard nothing, not even the cries of the Utes closing in on him.

Wheeling back to Nana, he saw the Apache struggle against the impaling limb. Bright red blood spurted from the wound, staining the snow. His black hair lay plastered to his face. Slade started to dismount, but the war cry of the Utes stayed him.

Anger boiled Slade's Indian blood. He

turned his steel gray eyes on the fast approaching Utes who waved their rifles over their heads in wild exultation. A bloodlust thirst for revenge coursed through his veins. His head spun.

He grabbed the Ute carbine, a battered Henry, from its case under the cinch and fired. The slug went wide. Slade adjusted. His next three shots knocked three Utes from their saddles, causing the remainder to pull up and, as he continued firing, retreat to the top of the slope where they milled about uncertainly.

Slade paused. He lowered his rifle and jumped to the ground, taking care to hold on to the reins so his pony wouldn't spook. He laid his hand on Nana's arm. With each beat of the Apache's heart, blood spurted from around the blackened limb protruding from his back.

Nana's eyes fluttered open, then closed.

Slade whispered urgently, "Be still. I'll take care of you."

Nana tried to smile. Blood ran down his chin. He shook his head.

"No," cried Slade. "You can't leave go like this. I won't let you." He dug his fingers into Nana's shoulders as if to pull his brother back from the beginning of his long journey to live with his father and his father's fathers.

Nana clutched Slade's hand. He squeezed once, then he died.

Slade laid his fingers against Nana's still warm throat. No blood coursed through his veins for a pulse, and no blood spurted from the injury. The young half-breed's head spun as if all that had happened were a dream. It was impossible. His boyhood friend, his brother, was dead.

The Ute cries caught his attention. At the top of the hill, they were massing for another attack. Enraged, Slade threw his rifle to his shoulder and touched off three more shots, which scattered the already nervous Indians. Their horses reared and jittered about.

Common sense told Slade that he could not stand and fight the Utes. Despite his anger and lust for revenge, one man against nine or ten was foolish. Reluctantly, Slade turned and disappeared into the forest, hoping that the Utes would pursue. To his disappointment, they didn't.

Satisfied with the dead Apache, they turned back to their own dead, leaving three Utes just inside the forest to watch over Nana's body just in case Slade returned.

From deep in a stand of cedar on the crest of the next slope, Slade watched the Utes retreat. He felt numb, like his insides had been ripped out. Finally, he turned back into the forest, unsure of just where he was going, moving on instinct, which told him that he had to find someplace he could hold against the Utes if they should decide to attack.

Just before dusk, he found a cave large enough for a small fire and space enough to picket his horse. The entrance overlooked a narrow valley, the only access to the cave. Too stunned to think about food or warmth, Slade camped cold.

Later that night, Slade built a small fire and stared into the flickering flames in a futile effort to sort his feelings. On the one hand, he wanted to hunt down the Utes and take his revenge for Nana. The more he thought about Nana, the more his fury fueled his rage.

He checked his .44 and then the Henry, preparing to chase down the Utes and make them pay. Then he could go back to Texas. But when he thought about Texas, he remembered Bent. The old man was waiting for Slade to return and free him.

But Slade didn't have the evidence to free Bent. He could not prove that Bent was innocent. And even if the Mormons were pleased with the money their herd brought, that would not be enough for them to free Bent.

He tried to convince himself that without evidence, there was no way he could help Bent by returning. He told himself that he might as well run down the Utes responsible for Nana's death; then he could bury his brother rather than leave him for the animals. At least he would gain that satisfaction.

All night he struggled with the decision.

During the early morning hours, he dozed. Just before sunrise, a whippoorwill call awakened him — or had it been only a dream? Slade cocked his ears for the coo of the dove, but the plaintive cry never came. It must have been only a dream. There were no whippoorwills up here, not this time of year. Whippoorwills wintered to the south.

But the call brought back memories of his youth, the games, the trials, the training. He could still hear the stern voice of Mangas Coloradas reminding them that the Apaches were the only true human beings, brave in battle and honorable in life.

The words had puzzled Slade at the time for he had always figured that he was a true human being even though he was part white, part Indian. But life among the white men and other Indians sometimes made him wonder if there was not more wisdom in the old chief's words than Slade gave him credit for. Many white men certainly did not meet his own concept of human beings. However, he reminded himself, thinking of the Utes, there were some Indians that didn't act like human beings either.

Later, still undecided as to his next move, Slade saddled his pony, pausing to double-check the cinch and stuff some more grass in the soft pad saddle. It was too loose, bringing to his lips a smile at the time Nana had taken a bad tumble because he had failed to check his cinch. Slade's smile faded into serious concentration as he remembered how the youth was reprimanded by the old chief and reminded that in battle, an Apache depended on no one but himself. If a brave falls, the other warriors do not return. If a brave cannot keep up, the others will not slow their pace.

That philosophy was the reason behind the twenty-mile runs, behind the desert training, behind the deliberate privations. That disciplined philosophy was the reason General George Crook would later call the Apache the "Tiger of the Southwest."

Slade knew then what he must do. He tightened his cinch and headed for Texas. The snow had fallen all night, a light breeze pushing it into gentle drifts. He paused at the crest of the last ridge for one final look at the lump of snow that was the body of his brother still impaled on the limb. He could not afford the time to bury him. For all he knew, the Utes were still lying in ambush awaiting his return.

No. First, he had to save Bent. Then he would return to bury his brother and take out his vengeance on the Utes.

CHAPTER
TWENTY-FOUR

Slade paused on the rim of the canyon, looking down on the neat community sprawled along the southern bank of the Canadian River. The sun was low and shadows cast by the canyon rim crawled across the valley.

One thing to say for those Mormons, he told himself, they were hard workers. Their village was clean, their homes in good repair, their late-autumn crops well tended.

The pastoral scene before him reminded Slade of a painting he had seen in a cannon-shelled antebellum mansion back during the War of Secession. The mansion was deserted. The porch had collapsed on itself, but its once stately columns remained standing, silent mourners of a dead culture. The windows were shattered, and the back walls of the old mansion had been blown away.

Inside, the painting of the mansion at the

height of its grace and glory hung askew on floral wallpaper. Taken by the splendor emanating from the painting, Slade found the contradiction of beauty and war disturbing.

And now as he looked down over the valley, he had the same disturbed feeling. The beauty of the community hid an ugliness, an intolerance, a prejudice toward those from outside. Hatred existed in New Gideon. Invisible, subtle, the hatred hid behind beliefs and within religious values, which excluded outsiders. One set of laws for the Saints, one set for heathens.

Hold on, Slade reminded himself, thinking of Jacob Ware. Not all of them viewed their religion the same way. There were some good ones, ones that treated everyone the same. It's just like most places, he decided. Seemed like the bad ones always outnumbered the good ones. Or at least, made themselves better known, or shouted louder.

Slade dug his heels into the pony's flank, suddenly filled with an urgency to reach the village. As he drew closer, a dark object on the outskirts of town began taking shape. Slade frowned. A sudden chill came over him. He forced it aside. But as he drew closer to the village, the bulky object came into focus, chilling the young half-breed's blood.

"Dammit," he muttered, viewing the gallows constructed of freshly sawn oak timbers.

Slade suppressed the sudden anger heating his blood and burning his cheeks. He would do nothing until he talked to the big blacksmith. Not even this group of Mormons would have been foolish enough to hang Bent before Slade returned.

But what if they had? What if they had listened to Aaron Smith? What if they believed the contemptible hatred the man espoused? He shook his head and muttered harshly, trying to convince himself, "Joseph Ware would have stopped it."

But deep down, Slade wondered if the blacksmith could head off a lynching. He would certainly pay no heed to Aaron Smith, but the others would. Most folks could be led even though they weren't sure where they were headed or why they were going. He had seen it among the Indians as well as the whites. All it took was some jasper with a hatred supported by imagination and a loud voice.

That being the case, people would flock to Aaron Smith and his ideas like geese to grain.

As Slade rode into town, he glimpsed a pale face peering out the window of Constance Young's house. The face jerked back behind the curtains. He shrugged it off, figuring the person in the house to be the woman herself.

He shook his head. The poor woman was a couple pickles shy of a full barrel, but she was a good woman. It wasn't her fault the good Lord didn't provide her the sense others had. Suddenly he saw Constance Young coming down the street toward him. For a moment, he wondered about the face in the window, then shoved it from his mind. Probably Sarah Cook.

Slade tipped his hat as he rode past her. He fixed his eyes on Joseph Ware's neat house. Slade rode down the street, hearing the scrape of doors opening and feeling eyes on his back. A low mutter of voices followed him as the menfolks poured from their doors and into the broad streets.

Slade stopped in front of Ware's house. He remained in the saddle and called out, "Ware!"

Moments later, Joseph Ware peered out the window. His eyes grew wide, and he jerked back.

Slade's breath came faster. From the corner of his eyes, he saw the crowd halt several feet away, forming a semicircle around him. Where was the blacksmith? Afraid to face Slade? Had they already hanged Bent?

The muscles in Slade's jaw rippled.

No one in the crowd spoke.

The door opened suddenly, and Three-Fingers Bent stepped onto the porch. "Howdy, boy. We's figurin' someone might have to go look for you."

Slade's shoulders slumped, and a grin creased his weathered face. "You all right?"

"As rain, boy. These folks been treatin' me right nice. Were it not for the trial an' all, I'd be as happy as a puppy with two tails."

"They been busy," Slade said sarcastically, nodding to the gallows on the outskirts of town.

Bent grunted. "I reckon they built it for me, but a couple days ago they hung that rustler we caught down at the river on it, about the time his leg had healed. Said they couldn't hang no hurt man. Had to get him well first, then hang him." He shook his head, a wry grin on his craggy face. "I still ain't got that figured out."

Ware followed Bent onto the porch. He held up a big hand in welcome. "Light and come on in. Mrs. Ware's laying out an extra place now. We'd about given up on you."

The wiry young man nodded. "Soon as I put up my horse."

"Hold on."

Aaron Smith stepped up on the porch. His craggy face reminded Slade of lightning and thunder. "Where's our cattle?"

Slade reached under his shirt and removed the money belt. He tossed it to Smith. "Sold at Raton Pass over in New Mexico Territory. We caught him too late, but here's the money."

Smith caught the belt. Slade continued. "According to your figures, you lost a couple hundred head. There's twenty-two hundred in the belt."

Garth Smith stepped up beside his father. He pushed his hat on the back of his head. "What about Bledsoe? What did you find out about his murder?" His voice was a sneer.

Slade studied the young man for several seconds. "Nothing. The one jasper who knew was John Daughtery, but the Utes had already skinned and killed him by the time we got to him."

"So," Garth Smith said. "You got no proof that Bent there didn't kill Wiley Bledsoe?"

Joseph Ware broke in. "There's none that he did, Garth Smith."

Smith's sneer broadened. "Then I think

it's time to get on with the trial. The judge will be swinging through here in two days on his way back from Fort Bascom."

Slade's muscles tensed as Garth Smith pointed an accusing finger at Bent. "We've treated this killer like a houseguest for the last month. It's time to make him pay for what he done to Wiley Bledsoe. I —"

Slade already had one leg over the saddle when Aaron Smith stopped his son. "That's enough, Garth."

"But, Pa —"

Aaron Smith roared, "I said, that's enough. We'll make no judgments. That is what the courts are for."

"But, Pa. You been sayin' that —"

The elder Smith glared at his offspring. "I said, that's enough."

Slade settled back into his saddle, his steel gray eyes fixed on Aaron Smith. Anger burned a hole in his stomach. "The apple don't fall too far from the tree, does it, Smith?"

"What's that you say?"

"You heard me."

Smith's face reddened. "Just what do you mean by that?"

"What I said. They grow up the way you train 'em, no worse, no better."

Aaron Smith coughed. "I'm not used to

being spoken to in such a manner. I —"

Slade's temper, on a short rein for the last few weeks, exploded. "Well, now, I reckon that's just too damned bad. We'll see just how —"

Joseph Ware intervened. "Hold on, both of you. Slade, go put up your horse and come inside. Aaron, you and your son go on home." The blacksmith raised his voice to the rest of the crowd. "That goes for all of you. Go on home. We'll finish this in the morning."

Aaron Smith's eyes flashed angrily. "Nobody talks like that to me, Joseph. You —"

Joseph Ware stepped forward, his mighty biceps bulging against the constraints of the cotton shirt he wore. There was fire-tempered steel in his voice when he spoke. "Aaron, you get yourself and your son home. I'm not saying it again." He looked at the crowd. "And I'm not telling the rest of you again."

Reluctantly, the crowd dispersed.

The blacksmith nodded to Slade. "You know where the barn is. Wash up and come eat."

Noting that the Slade had lost weight, Mrs. Ware heaped his plate to overflowing with homemade biscuits and gravy, greens, and a thick steak. She set a bowl of plum jelly by the biscuits as Joseph Ware explained how the judge had decided to push on to Fort Bascom and then swing back by New Gideon.

Slade eyed the fare ravenously. The days on the trail had been thin on solid grub. He would do his dead level best to make up for the poor quality and quantity of trail chow.

But Bent's first question killed Slade's appetite. "Where'd Nana camp?"

Slade lowered his knife and fork to his plate. He stared at the utensils for several seconds before lifting his eyes and fixing them on Bent's. He felt his eyes burn, and in a voice tight with emotion, the leather-tough young man muttered, "He's dead." And in a voice choked with emotion, he told Bent and Ware what had taken place.

No one spoke when he finished. Ware balled his great hands into fists. Bent rubbed a gnarled knuckle into one eye. Slade rose slowly and walked outside.

Ware started after him, but Bent stopped the blacksmith. "Let him go."

"I can be there if he wants to talk about it," Ware replied.

Bent shook his head. "There's enough Injun in Jake that he'll find the answer by hisself." He nodded to Ware's empty glass.

295

"Have another glass of milk. I never thought I'd say so, but I reckon I've taken a fancy to milk."

Ware plopped back down in his chair as his wife bustled over and filled their glasses. She returned to the kitchen where she busied herself straightening the room before bedtime. A few minutes later she returned, a heaping plate covered with a white linen napkin in her hands. "Open the door, Joseph. Mr. Slade's headed for the barn. He'll be hungry sooner or later."

CHAPTER
TWENTY-FIVE

The night seemed endless. Although he was exhausted from the trail, Slade could not sleep. Nana's death and his own inability to prove Bent's innocence nagged at him. His eyes burned from lack of sleep, but every time he began to nod off, he remembered Bent.

He had to find something. He couldn't let Bent die. Not after Nana gave his life for the cantankerous old man. But where to turn? What could he do? During the early morning hours, Slade made up his mind. He had always tried to abide by the law, but if this kangaroo court found Bent guilty, Slade would take the law into his own hands and break his old friend out of jail.

Bent would never hang.

A tight smile lit his face. Hell, if he and Bent didn't pull it off, at least they would go out together. Besides, they had two days before the judge arrived. Anything could happen. And with those grim thoughts in mind, Slade dropped into a fitful slumber.

To Slade's surprise and consternation, the judge arrived early the next morning from Fort Bascom. Bent's trial was set for two o'clock that afternoon.

"And we'll see the gallows used once again before dark," Slade overheard one of the villagers say to a group of the Saints in front of the Council Hall.

The remainder of the morning Slade spent in the barn, checking rigging, making sure his and Bent's horses were fed and watered. They would have to ride hard when the time came.

He was cleaning rocks from his horse's shoes when a shadow appeared in the open door. Slade glanced up. Joseph Ware filled the opening. His square face was rock hard. "You've been looking after those animals mighty careful-like this morning, Jake."

The young half-breed dropped the hoof and wiped the blade of his knife on his worn denims. "Never can tell when a soul might need them, Joseph." He slid the knife back in its sheath.

The blacksmith looked over the saddles and other gear, all freshly cleaned and ready for use. "You're not planning on nothing foolish, are you, Jake?"

Slade grinned. "You ought to know me better'n that. I'm a peaceable man." He hesitated, then added, "What if I was though? What would you do, Joseph?"

Joseph Ware didn't reply. For several seconds, the two men stared into each other's eyes, each appraising the other. The big blacksmith dropped his gaze first. "The law is the law. We got to abide by it even if we don't want to."

"Even if a body knows it's wrong, Joseph?"

Slowly the blacksmith nodded. "Even if it's wrong."

Slade's grin broadened. "Well, I can't say as I agree with you but don't worry. If I decide to do something wrong, you'll be the first to know."

After the big blacksmith left, Slade headed across town to see Sarah Cook. He had been considering Bent's case. The most incriminating evidence was the twenty-dollar gold piece found beside Wiley Bledsoe. The young girl was the only one he knew to possess such a coin, the one Bent had given her to assist her effort to leave the small village and start over elsewhere.

Slade had wanted to believe her when she told him that the coin was missing the next morning. He still wanted to believe her. He could be wrong, but for the life of him, he couldn't picture her as the killer. Still, he had to know for certain.

Most people have trouble remembering lies, and sometimes the right question, dropped as an afterthought, trips them. Slade hoped the theory was true. If she had lied, maybe when he questioned her today, she would contradict her original story.

If she were telling the truth, then the disappearance of the coin meant that someone had entered Constance Young's small house and deliberately stolen the coin to place the blame on Bent. Or Constance Young herself had taken it for the same reason.

The last speculation was an afterthought, and a foolish one at that, he told himself. What reason could a crazy woman have for murdering Wiley Bledsoe?

He shook his head, rejecting the idea as ludicrous. Besides, the size of the indistinct footprints outside the window indicated that the murderer was a man.

Still, used as evidence at the trial, the questions could raise a reasonable doubt. But only with reasonable folks, Slade reminded himself bitterly. These Mormons weren't any too reasonable.

He turned off the broad street onto the

narrow one that led to Constance Young's. To his surprise, he saw Sarah Cook heading down the street in his direction.

He took off his hat as they drew near. "Morning."

Her eyes sparkled. "Good morning, Mr. Slade. I heard you were back."

He smiled wryly. "Bad news travels fast."

She chided him. "You're not bad news, Mr. Slade. Why, I'd think that you would be good news. You brought the money back."

"Well, at least something good came of it." He hesitated, uncertain just how he would ask her once again about the coin without her believing that he suspected her. "Everything fine with you?"

She nodded. "Very well, thank you. I'm living with the Webbs now. I moved in with them just after you left. They're fine people. And I'm saving my money. Soon I'll have enough to leave. Maybe on to Los Angeles." She hesitated and glanced around. "I just wish I hadn't lost that gold coin Mr. Bent gave me."

"It would have come in handy," he said, jumping at the opening she had provided. "Too bad you didn't put it up someplace for safekeeping," he added with an air of indifference.

She corrected him. "Oh, no, but I did. I

301

told you. Don't you remember? I put it in my keepsake tin on my nightstand. I'm certain of that now. I've thought a lot about it in the last weeks."

The young girl paused and stared into Slade's gray eyes. "You believe me, don't you?"

Suddenly, Slade did believe her. "Yeah. I do."

Her eyes shone and her cheeks flushed. "I'm glad. I really thought hard about it. I know for sure I put it in the tin box on my nightstand. I —"

Slade interrupted as her earlier words registered in his brain. "The Webbs? You're not living with Miss Young?"

Her forehead knitted in a frown. "No. I said a minute ago that I'd been living with the Webbs since a day or two after you left."

He didn't answer. He was suddenly curious as to the identity of the person peering through Constance Young's window when he rode in the day before. "Did you visit Miss Young anytime yesterday."

She pursed her lips. "Why, yes —" Slade relaxed. So it *was* her. "Yesterday morning, just after sunrise."

After sunrise? "What about yesterday afternoon late?"

She shook her head. "No. I didn't go back.

Yesterday morning, she acted like I was intruding or something. She wouldn't let me inside. She's been like that since a few days after I moved out. You see, I'd come to borrow some flour for Mrs. Webb." She paused. "You know, it's strange. Used to be, Miss Young was real friendly, but like I said, in the last weeks, she's changed."

"Changed? How?"

Sarah Cook studied over the question before answering. "I don't know exactly. She just don't visit as much like she once did. Stays to herself more, if you know what I mean." She glanced at the sun. "Oh, dear. I'm late. I've got to hurry." She threw him a broad smile. "Good-bye, Mr. Slade."

He tipped his hat. "Good morning, Miss Cook." He recollected her last remark about Constance Young. *Stays to herself more, if you know what I mean.* Like she had something to hide, the young half-breed told himself. But what? Could it have something to do with Wiley Bledsoe? No. He would sooner believe that Geronimo had taken to growing sweet corn than believe Constance Young had anything to do with the murder. Strange how the guilty can always look so free of wrongdoing, and the innocent so guilty.

Still, Constance Young's sudden seclusion

was puzzling. He remembered Joseph telling him how Mrs. Ware always complained over the addled woman's unexpected and lengthy visits. What could have happened to make her change?

He shrugged off the question, figuring she was like everyone else, just growing older, more forgetful, less patient. The wiry young man had a more important question to answer. He had to decide if he should reveal the evidence against Sarah Cook at Bent's trial even though he was convinced of her innocence.

Knowing the mindset of some of the folks in the village, they might jump up and put her on trial. But she was no more guilty than Bent. With a groan, Slade figured he might as well try to save Bent as her. At least he and Bent could hightail it out of town if the verdict came in wrong. What could Sarah Cook do?

CHAPTER
TWENTY-SIX

While waiting for the Bent's escort to the Council Hall, Slade slipped out to the barn and saddled his Indian pony and Bent's bay. He clacked cartridges into the chambers of the Henry he had taken from the Utes and Bent's Winchester before slipping them into their scabbards. Having been informed after their first meeting in the Council Hall that firearms were not worn in court, Slade shoved a spare revolver under his belt and tucked in his shirt over it. If they had to make a break, he wanted to be sure they had firepower.

Just before two o'clock, three members of the Stake High Council called for Bent. Reluctantly, Slade unfastened his gun belt and draped it over the back of a chair.

The day was unusually warm for autumn. The sun beamed down from a sky free of clouds, baking the street into dust that billowed up about their feet at each step.

Far to the northeast, another cloud of dust rose from the canyon rim. But no one noticed, for all eyes in New Gideon were fixed on the Council Hall.

The hall was packed. The Stake officers, Joseph Ware, Aaron Smith, and Caleb Webb sat in the first row. The thirteen members of the Stake High Council sat in the second, and the men and boys of New Gideon filled the remainder of the pews.

On the dais in the front of the hall, a somber judge with thick muttonchop sideburns on his slablike face sat behind the same gate-legged table the Stake High Council used. His hair was thick and gray, growing like wild grass in every direction. His lips curled down into a perpetual frown. Next to the table was a straight-backed chair for the witnesses.

A murmur arose as Bent's entourage entered. A man by the back door looked at Joseph Ware. The blacksmith cast a hidden glance at Slade, then nodded. The man disappeared out the door.

Slade had just lost one of his hole cards.

The murmuring grew louder until Bent and Slade took their places behind a small table before the judge. With a sharp rap of his gavel, the judge silenced the room.

Slade looked at Bent. He had agreed to

serve as lawyer for his old friend. He just hoped that the judge was fair-minded, not given to letting conjecture cloud his decision like many of the judges Slade had the misfortune of observing.

When the room grew silent, the imposing figure at the front of the room spoke in a booming voice. "My name is Judge Frank Mayhall. I've read the accusation. Who's in charge of the prosecution?"

Joseph Ware rose and introduced himself. "I'm the Stake President here, Your Honor, and it is normally my job to speak against the one on trial. But if the court don't mind, I'd like to turn that job over to one of the counselors, Aaron Smith."

"I've no objections, Mr. Ware."

"And, your Honor. I'd like to lend a hand in helping Mr. Bent." He nodded at the table before the judge. "He's the one on trial for killing Wiley Bledsoe."

Judge Mayhall nodded. "Again, I've no objection if nobody else around here does." He glanced over the room. No one spoke. "Good. Now, let's get on with it."

A sense of relief washed over Slade. Ware was better with words than he was, and he was one of New Gideon's own. Maybe that would work to Bent's advantage.

Aaron Smith called his first witness, Caleb Webb.

Under Smith's questioning, Webb briefly related the first visit with Slade and Bent in this very room.

"And after Mr. Bent struck Wiley Bledsoe, what happened then?"

Webb nodded to Bent. "Then the defendant there pulled his gun on us, and then they took you and me hostage so they could get to their horses."

Aaron Smith pursed his lips. "And was anything said between Mr. Slade and the defendant?"

"Yep. Mr. Slade said 'let's go,' and then Mr. Bent said 'I got me a spanking new twenty-dollar gold piece that says we don't make it.' "

"Are you sure he said 'spanking new'?"

"Positive."

Slade frowned at Bent as Aaron Smith stepped to the judge's table and picked up a gold coin and handed it to Caleb Webb.

"Like this?"

Webb studied it and nodded. "Yep. 1870. And it looks as new to me as a wobbly-legged little heifer." He handed it back to Aaron Smith.

A murmur spread through the room as men glanced at each other and nodded.

Bent shifted in his chair and glanced at Slade.

"Then what happened?"

Webb pointed out the window in the direction of Ware's barn. "You know what happened, Aaron. You was there."

Aaron Smith nodded. "I know, Caleb, but Judge Mayhall here would like to hear about it."

Webb's cheeks colored. He nodded at the judge. "Sorry, Judge. Well, they took us to the barn. Then they rode off." He looked back to Aaron Smith. "That's it."

"Thank you, Caleb," said Aaron Smith. He turned to the judge. "I got no more questions for the witness, Your Honor."

Joseph Ware rose quickly. "I got me one or two, Your Honor."

Mayhall nodded, and the big blacksmith stepped around the table and faced Caleb Webb. "Caleb, I reckon every man in New Gideon heard Mr. Bent make that remark about the gold piece. Don't you reckon so?"

Caleb Webb nodded. "All that was there heard him."

Ware glanced around the room. "Tell me, Caleb. You ever take a belt to your son?"

Caleb Webb frowned and looked to the judge.

Mayhall said to Ware, "I don't see what

309

that question has to do with the trial, Mr. Ware."

"Please, Your Honor. It goes right to the heart of the matter."

The judge nodded. "Answer the question, Mr. Webb."

"I reckon ever' man here has."

The blacksmith nodded. "And they usually deserved it, I've no doubt. Don't you think so?"

"I wouldn't of done it if the boy hadn't."

"You ever get real mad and say something to him like 'I'm going to flay the hide off your back, boy'?"

Caleb Webb shrugged. "I reckon I have." With a crooked grin, he added, "Reckon everybody here has."

A ripple of chuckles spread through the audience.

Ware continued. "But you didn't really mean that you were really going to peel his skin, did you?"

A glimmer of suspicion arched Caleb Webb's brows. "No," he replied.

"Did you see Mr. Bent's twenty-dollar gold piece?"

"I seen it after they found it by Wiley Bledsoe."

"That's not what I asked, Caleb. I asked if you ever saw Mr. Bent holding that gold piece in his own hand."

Caleb Webb squirmed. He glanced at Aaron Smith, and then at the judge.

"I'm waiting, Caleb. Did you ever see Mr. Bent with the twenty-dollar gold piece in his hand?"

Caleb Webb's eyes narrowed. "No."

"Then how do you know it was his?"

"Because he said so."

The blacksmith shook his head. "No. He said the words, 'I got me a spanking new twenty-dollar gold piece says we don't make it'. Ain't that right?"

"It's the same thing. Why would he have said it if he didn't mean it?"

"Why do you tell your boy you're going to peel his hide when you don't mean it?"

Caleb Webb shook his head. "That's just talk."

Joseph Ware nodded and looked at the judge. "And that's all Mr. Bent's words was, your Honor — just talk, like Caleb's here. They wasn't meant to be took serious. It was just an expression he used." He looked at Bent and added with a wry grin, "In the days Mr. Bent has spent in my house, your Honor, I've come to see he uses a lot of different expressions. Many that are not too pleasant on my ears."

Slade leaned back in his chair and grinned

at Bent.

Outside, the cloud of dust drew closer to New Gideon as Judge Mayhall considered Ware's argument. He picked up the coin and studied it. After several moments, he cleared his throat. "Mr. Ware. Do you have a twenty-dollar gold piece?"

The blacksmith stood. "No, sir."

Judge Mayhall looked around the room. "Anyone here have a twenty-dollar gold piece?"

Aaron Smith spoke for all. "No, sir. Mostly we barter, but sometimes we have to go outside and make purchases, and even then we do that through the bank. Around here, we have no need to carry money around with us. We got no traffic passing through 'cause we're off the main trail, and we have few visitors other than occasions such as this one. In fact, the money we found at Wiley Bledsoe's was probably the most any of us have seen since our trip to Fort Dodge last year."

"You mean to tell me you people have not been out of this valley in over a year?"

"No reason to, Your Honor," said Caleb Webb. "We supply all we need to live on."

The judge nodded and studied the coin in his hand. He cleared his throat and spoke in a soft, conversational tone as if he were explaining an idea to an old friend. "One hobby of mine is numismatics, which is the study of currency and coins." He held the gold coin up for all to see. "The date on this coin is 1870, which in itself might not mean a great deal, for over seven hundred thousand of these gold pieces have been minted so far this year."

A sudden apprehension tensed Slade's muscles. He didn't know what the judge had in mind, but whatever it was, Slade had the feeling it was bad news. He leaned forward.

Judge Mayhall continued. "But what is intriguing is the location of the mint where this coin was made. This particular coin is an 1870 CC, which means it was minted in Carson City, this year."

He hesitated and fixed his eyes on Three-Fingers Bent. "What is so incriminating about this coin is that less than three thousand of them have been minted in Carson City to date. Consequently, it is a rarity."

Slade's hand slid inside his shirt as he waited for Judge Mayhall to finish his comments.

"And since nobody has left this valley in over a year, I can see no way for the coin to come to New Gideon except by strangers."

He paused and looked at Joseph Ware. "Mister Ware. How many visitors have you folks in New Gideon had within the past year? Besides these two," he added.

The blacksmith stared at the table before him.

"Mr. Ware?" The judge prompted him.

Reluctantly, Joseph Ware looked up.

"How many, Mr. Ware?"

Slade's fingers tightened on his revolver.

Joseph Ware shook his head slowly. "None, Your Honor. But that don't prove nothing. Someone coulda had one stuck back somewhere, and they might —"

The crack of the gavel interrupted Ware. "No, Mr. Ware. This coin came in with these two men. There can be no question." He stared at Bent. "Mr. Bent, you will rise for the verdict of the court."

Jerking his revolver from under his shirt, Slade leaped to his feet. "Hold it right there, Judge." In three quick steps, Slade was behind the judge. He looked across the room. "Just everyone stay where he is. Nobody'll get hurt. Come on up here, Bent."

"Mr. Slade. What you are doing is a felony, punishable by imprisonment."

"You've got to catch us first, Judge."

Ware stepped forward. "Put it down, Jake.

You've got no place to run."

Slade grinned. "Just out of Texas is all, Joseph."

The blacksmith shook his head. "Your horses are gone, Jake."

The young half-breed stared at Ware. "What are you talking about?"

"I had them moved with the others over to the river."

Slade recognized the truth in Ware's somber face. "But why? Why'd you do that to us, Joseph?"

"I figured you'd try something like this if the verdict went against Bent. I don't want no more killing than necessary."

Slade's ears burned. "Well, then," he said, waving the muzzle of his .44. "Suppose you just send someone over there and bring them back unless you want a taste of .44."

Ware shook his head. "You're not that kind of man, Jake. You won't kill without being pushed into it."

"Maybe you're right, but I reckon you're doing a hell of a job pushing right now."

"No, I'm not, Jake, but we're going to stand right here until you put that gun down."

"Then you'll have a hell of a long wait, 'cause I'm not about to put it down." Slade glanced at Bent. "Follow me. We're getting

315

out of here." He turned back to the crowd of men who had moved a step closer. "Now, you men just stand aside. We're coming through."

The men glanced at each other, then reluctantly began moving aside.

"No. You men stay where you are," yelled Joseph Ware.

The men froze and stared at Slade.

"Damn you, Joseph. You're going to get someone killed. I said we're coming through, and that's exactly what we're going to do." He extended his arm and aimed at the floor just in front of the crowd.

CHAPTER
TWENTY-SEVEN

"Hold it, son." Three-Fingers Bent spoke up, his voice low and deep.

Slade hesitated, his eyes remaining on the crowd. "What do you want?"

"This ain't going to accomplish nothing. You got a chance to get out of here. I don't reckon they'll do nothing to you if you just back off. You kill someone, and they'll hunt you for life."

Slade shook his head. "We're getting out of here and heading back to Arizona Territory." Bitterly, he added, "Let them try to find us up in the Superstitions."

He felt Bent's bony hand on his shoulder. "Put the gun down, Jake. We got caught bluffing, so let's fold our hands and let them do what they want."

The young half-breed's head reeled. First Nana, now Bent. He felt the anger racing through his veins. "I'm not bluffing."

He extended his left arm out to his side

and stepped backward, forcing Bent back to the window. The crowd muttered and took a step forward. "Hold it," he said, his voice ominous with warning.

Slade glanced out the window. All they had to do was climb out the window, run to the river, and mount their horses. A grim smile tugged at his thin lips. They had as much chance of doing all that as bulldog-ging a buffalo. But he damned well was go-ing to try. Bent had been like a father to Slade, and the young half-breed would die trying to do all he could to save the cantan-kerous old man.

"The window," he muttered, his eyes play-ing over the crowded hall.

He heard the sliding of the window as Bent raised it. At the rear of the room, one of the men reached for the back door. Slade fired.

The slug smashed into the top of the door, tearing a gaping hole in the wood and rip-ping it out of the man's hands. "Nobody goes outside," Slade said loud enough for the entire body to hear. "I've got five slugs left."

"You can't get us all," a voice called out from the middle of the crowd.

"Maybe not, but I can get five of you." Slade backed to the window and glanced outside. He froze.

Peering from the window of Constance Young's house was Joe Rearden, the young rustler Slade had befriended in the Daughtery gang. When Joe Rearden saw Slade, he ducked behind the curtain.

Suddenly, all of the pieces fell into place for Slade as well as the answer to the question he never thought to ask — the question that had been nagging at him for the last several weeks, the question he had been unable to form. Bent was poised to climb out the window when the young half-breed called out, "Hold on, Bent."

The older man looked over his shoulder, his eyes questioning the younger man.

"Come on back in."

The crowd hesitated, puzzled by the sudden turnaround of the young half-breed.

Bent didn't move. Slade said, "I think I just figured out who stabbed Wiley Bledsoe to death."

A collective gasp escaped from the crowd as Slade turned to Judge Mayhall. "You can do what you want to with me later, Your Honor. But right now, I'm going to prove Bent didn't kill Wiley Bledsoe. I think a woman killed him. I'm not exactly sure why, but I'm going to get the answer right now." He nodded outside. "I'll be back, but you

319

can send a couple men with me if you don't trust me."

"What about Mr. Bent?"

"He's staying here."

The judge grunted, "Then I'll let you go by yourself. How long will you need?"

"No more than five minutes."

"I'll time you," Judge Mayhall said, retrieving his pocket watch from his vest.

Before the five minutes were up, a burst of gunfire erupted outside the hall. Moments later, the door flew open, and Slade staggered in, hauling a young man over his shoulder.

"Quick, shut the door," he said, lowering the limp man to the floor.

Several slugs splintered the door.

"What's going on out there," demanded Judge Mayhall.

"Part of Daughtery's gang. The rustlers," said Slade, rising and nodding to the unconscious young man on the floor with the blood seeping from his shoulder. "Four of them. Looks like they come here to make sure this young feller keeps his mouth closed. They just rode up, and the one they call Kansas Jack shot him."

Joseph Ware bent over Joe Rearden and tried to stem the flow of blood.

Another burst of gunfire ripped holes in the door and shattered the glass in the windows. As one, all the men dropped to the floor. Wild yells echoed through the streets as a continuous barrage of lead punched hole after hole in the doors and windows of the Council Hall.

Moving in a crouch, Slade removed Rearden's gun belt and strapped it on. He cursed when he saw that the revolver was a ball and cap. He checked the cylinder before tossing it to Bent. "You only got six shots."

He glanced at Joseph Ware. "Too bad about your rule on firearms. We could sure use a couple Winchesters about now," he said above the roaring of the pistols and the splattering lead tearing through the walls.

Ware smiled ruefully and returned to tending Joe Rearden.

Slade peered over the windowsill at the riders. He counted three. Firing came from the other side of the town hall. That was the location of the fourth owlhoot.

Suddenly the firing ceased. A voice called out, "Hey, you in there. The one named Slade. You hear me?"

"Yeah, I hear you. What do you want?"

"The kid. That's all. Send him out, and we'll ride off."

"Forget it, Jack. He stays with me. You

321

best hightail it out of here while you can." As Slade spoke, he set the front sights just above the shoulder of one of the gang. Slowly he squeezed the trigger as he said, "Otherwise, we'll make it mighty hot for you boys."

Just as his last words died away, he touched off the shot. The rider screamed as he was hurled from the saddle and slammed to the ground.

Before the echo died away, Jack grabbed his Winchester and leaped from his saddle and dashed into Constance Young's house. The other rustler spurred his horse and disappeared into the village.

An eerie silence settled over New Gideon.

Slade peered over the windowsill. The crack of a Winchester cut through the air. Slade jerked back against the wall as slivers of wood peppered his face.

Bent was at the front door, holding his fire and waiting for a sure target. They had ten cartridges between them, and in a heated battle, so a few went damned fast.

Kansas Jack and his remaining two men were in no such bind. Every few seconds, one of them fired, continually raking the Council Hall with 200-grain slugs.

Slade knew where Kansas Jack was holed up. Finally, he located the position of the second man. The outlaw was hiding behind the corner of a house a hundred feet south of Jack. Quickly, Slade crawled over to Bent.

"You got your man spotted?"

"Yep." The older man nodded to a barn west of them. "He's in there, back in the shadows," he said, indicating the dark interior of the barn.

Slade grinned tightly. The rustlers had left the north end of the town hall uncovered. "When I give you the sign, fire once or twice. I'm going out the back and try to come in on your man from behind."

Three-Fingers gave a terse nod. "Be careful, boy."

"I always am," he said over his shoulder as he turned away. He hesitated when he saw Joseph Ware looking at him. Slade forced a grin. The big blacksmith nodded.

At the rear of the town hall, Slade opened the door just a crack and peered outside. He grimaced. Damn these wide streets, he said to himself, noting that he had at least seventy-five feet of wide open space to cover before reaching the shelter of the building on the other side of the street.

Taking a deep breath, he nodded to Bent and slung open the door.

The old man opened fire.

Slade dashed into the street in a crouch,

expecting to feel the wrenching impact of a slug at every step. The ground at his feet exploded as a slug tore up the soil. Digging his toes into the ground, he cut sharply to one side, then back to the other, zigzagging across the street.

A slug tugged at his shirt as he ducked around the corner of a freshly whitewashed frame house. Pressing his back up against the wall, Slade glanced at his burning stomach. Blood stained his shirt.

He opened his shirt and breathed a sigh of relief. A red line creased the rippling muscles in his stomach. Only a flesh wound, but the sweat pouring into it caused it to burn like hell. Which, he thought to himself, is where I'd probably be now if that slug had been a couple inches back.

The firing continued, tearing chunks of wood from the corner of the house. From inside the Council Hall, Bent returned the fire once, then paused. Moments later, he fired again. The time between the shots told Slade that the old man was moving from door to window, trying to keep both sides busy.

Quickly, the young half-breed made his way between the houses to the rear of the barn, his ears tuned to the firing. The corrals enclosed a flat-roofed pole barn. A newer barn with steep gables at either end had later been built with one end attached to the pole barn.

Slade crouched behind a thick cotton-wood post, grateful now that Joseph Ware had ordered the horses taken to the river. Otherwise, the animals might have made Slade's presence known to the owlhoot within the barn.

Three sharp reports echoed from inside the cavernous structure. Winchester.

Slade palmed his .44. Crouching, he followed the corral to the back of the barn where he climbed through the rails and knelt by the rear door. He waited until the man inside began firing before slipping into one of the stalls along the side of the barn and hiding in the shadows cast by the feed trough at the end of the stall.

The air was cool and ripe with the musty smell of hay and sweetly pungent with the cloying odor of manure. He peered into the darkness of the barn.

The rustler fired again, the orange-red muzzle blasts revealing his position behind a stack of hay in the middle of the barn floor. Slade had a clear shot at him.

Not wanting to kill the man, Slade eased to his right, testing each step before he placed his weight on his foot. Like a wraith, he glided through the darkness until he came up behind the outlaw.

Suddenly the rustler spun, the Winchester at his hip angled up at Slade. The Indian in Slade reacted instinctively. He threw himself aside as both men fired. Slade hit the ground with a jolt and rolled over and fired again.

The Winchester roared again. Slade rolled to his right, still firing even as he rolled behind one of the stall walls. He waited.

The Winchester was silent.

He remained back in the darkness of the stall, knowing the shadows hid him. He strained his eyes to penetrate the dark barn. Nothing.

Outside, the firing continued.

Slade couldn't afford to wait any longer. Bent must be almost out of cartridges.

He eased forward, his finger tight on the trigger, his muscles bunched, ready to leap. He saw nothing, only the stack of hay. Moving to his left as silently as the mice that played in the barn, Slade strained his eyes against the darkness.

A dark object like a hoe handle lay on the ground protruding from behind the hay. Another step, and Slade made it out to be the barrel of the Winchester. Stooping quickly, he grabbed the hot barrel and spun it across the barn.

A darker figure lay in the shadows cast by the hay.

Slade knelt and touched his finger to the pulse in the man's neck. Nothing. He grimaced. But he had no time to waste. Taking the outlaw's gun belt and retrieving the Winchester, Slade headed back to the Council Hall, taking care to keep the building between him and the other two men.

Now, it was Kansas Jack's turn.

The additional weapons and cartridges were greeted with a sigh of relief from Bent. "I was down to my last ca'tridge," he said.

Slade gave Bent the Winchester, and Judge Mayhall took the outlaw's revolver. "Before I took up judging," he said when Slade arched an eyebrow in surprise, "I held four thousand acres of Texas prairie against Indians and carpetbaggers. I know what it's all about."

The young half-breed grinned. "I reckon you do, Judge."

Slade eased to the side of the window and called out. "Jack. It's me, Slade." He paused, then said, "We got your man in the barn. There's only two of you left, and you're next." He watched the house.

Moments later, a single set of hoofbeats raced south out of town.

"I reckon you heard that, Jack. Looks like you're the only one left now. What do you say?"

Aaron Smith stepped forward. "You say that man's one of the rustlers who stole our cattle?"

Slade glanced at the old man. "That's what I said."

"You act like you want him to escape." He looked at the judge. "Why don't you arrest that man out there, Your Honor? Then we can try him for rustling."

The judge studied Aaron Smith for several seconds while Slade watched, a wry grin on his face. "I tell you what, Mr. Smith," replied the judge, "I'll deputize you as a state marshal, and you go out there and arrest the man."

Aaron Smith sputtered. Before he could reply, the beat of hoofs sounded from the east.

Slade said, "There's goes Jack."

Mayhall grinned and slid the revolver under his belt and pulled his vest over it. "We'll get him later. That kind always gets caught. Now," he said, taking his place behind the table and reaching for his gavel, "Let's get the rest of this business settled." He nodded at Joe Rearden. "First, some of you men put this man in a bed where he can be looked after."

As three men carried Joe Rearden from the room, Slade left the hall and returned moments later carrying a pair of brogans as large as canoes. He dropped them on the table in front of the judge.

"What is this, Mr. Slade?"

"Evidence, Your Honor."

Judge Mayhall frowned. "You better explain yourself. Just who was that wounded man, and who killed Wiley Bledsoe?" He waved an impatient hand at the brogans. "And what do these have to do with the murder?"

Jake Slade looked around the room. "I was raised by the Indians, Your Honor. That was my family. Even when I did something wrong, they supported me. Oh, they corrected me, all right, and whatever I had done, I sure wouldn't do again. But they were a family to me."

Judge Mayhall interrupted. "I don't see what you're driving at."

"Just this, Judge. If I held anyone responsible for what happened to Wiley Bledsoe, it would be all of New Gideon."

Surprised murmurs spread over the room.

Aaron Smith jumped to his feet. "I resent that remark. He doesn't —"

Judge Mayhall gaveled him to silence.

"Continue, Mr. Slade."

"I know the town didn't do it, but folks did a lot of things that led up to all this. For example, the gold piece found beside Wiley Bledsoe was Bent's."

Judge Mayhall frowned. "What is that you're saying?"

Slade nodded. "That's right. Bent gave the coin to a young woman of this town to help her escape New Gideon because she was being treated so bad."

Mutters of disbelief arose from the crowd again. Judge Mayhall rapped his gavel. "I don't see your point, Mr. Slade. Do you know who killed Wiley Bledsoe? If you do, tell us his name."

Slade nodded. "All right, Your Honor, but it was not a man. It was a woman — I never thought to ask why Bledsoe was stabbed instead of clubbed or shot. That was a question that had been nagging at me, but I was too dense to see it. A revolver or a club is heavy and cumbersome in a woman's hands, but a woman can handle a knife with ease."

He paused and pointed at the brogans. "And she wore those boots to throw us off." He tossed one of the brogans to Ware. "Look at the heel, Joseph."

Ware turned the brogan over. With a thick finger, he touched the bent nail in the heel.

He looked at the judge. "This was the print outside Wiley Bledsoe's window, Judge."

Slade then pointed out the door through which Joe Rearden had disappeared. "I found the brogans in the home of Miss Constance Young, who I believe is not only Joe Rearden's mother, but the one who killed Wiley Bledsoe."

The crowd of men drew in a collective breath.

"Preposterous," yelled Aaron Smith. "She isn't married. And she could never hurt anyone. She might be addled, but she's harmless."

"Sit down and keep quiet, Mr. Smith," ordered the judge.

Slade continued. "The girl that Bent gave the coin once lived with Constance Young. Recently, she moved over to the Webbs'. While she slept, Constance Young took the coin —"

Judge Mayhall rapped his gavel. "Hold on, Mr. Slade. These are serious accusations against Miss Young, very serious. We will go no further until she is present to defend herself." He turned to Aaron Smith. "Go fetch her, Mr. Smith."

Twenty minutes later, Aaron Smith returned with Constance Young. "She was visiting Mrs. Ware when the shooting started. She was afraid to go home."

Constance Young's eyes played over the assembly of men nervously. When she reached the front of the room, Judge Mayhall spoke. "Miss Young, there have been some serious accusations made against you. It is only fair that you be present to hear them. Do you understand what I'm saying?"

She sat without replying. With her hands clasped in her lap, she nodded, her face an opaque mask of indifference.

The judge spoke to Slade. "Continue, Mr. Slade."

The young half-breed glanced at Constance Young with apology scribed across his face. He never had spoken against a woman. He didn't like the feeling, but he could see no choice.

As gently as possible, he repeated his accusations for her benefit, and then turned back to the judge. "At first, I didn't connect Miss Young with the missing coin. But too many unrelated things happened. Like that night when we rode into New Gideon after the rustlers. She told us that a couple hours earlier, she had seen a band of men riding south. That she had seen them in the starlight."

Joseph Ware spoke up. "I remember that, Your Honor."

Slade continued. "But, she couldn't have seen anything in the starlight like she said because the rain stopped and the cloud cover blew away just before we rode in. Two hours earlier, it was pouring rain."

Aaron Smith cleared his throat. "As much as I hate to admit it, Your Honor, he's right about that. I had visited my brother that night. The rain kept me at his house for two or three hours. When it cleared off, I headed home. I saw Slade and that Injun ride up to Joseph Ware's."

Constance Young sat motionless, her face showing no emotion.

"Something mighty important had happened to make her lie to her own kind," Slade said softly. "I'm not judging anybody for anything, certainly not Miss Young. What I figure is that Bledsoe was blackmailing her, threatening to tell the town she had a son. She was afraid if the town found out, she would be shunned, treated the same way this town treats Sarah Cook."

Aaron Smith cleared his throat uncomfortably. Garth Smith's cheeks burned with embarrassment.

"Why would he blackmail Miss Young?" Judge Mayhall's forehead wrinkled in a puzzled frown. "She had nothing to do with the cattle."

Slade shook his head. "The cattle had nothing to do with it. Wiley Bledsoe was the kind of man who would take from anyone. He blackmailed her because he saw the chance to make a few more dollars of crooked money to go with what he got as his share of the rustling."

"I see," replied the judge. "But can you prove that young boy is her son, Mr. Slade?"

Constance Young stiffened. She cut her eyes at Jake Slade, then dropped her gaze to her lap once again.

He could not prove she was Joe's mother. He knelt in front of her. "I was in the gang with Joe Rearden. That's when I heard that Bledsoe was the rustler's contact here in New Gideon and that a female done him in."

"Maybe you're not his ma," Slade said to the silent woman. "But you're the only one who could have taken the coin from Sarah Cook's jewelry box. I found the brogans in your house. You lied about seeing the rustlers, and the rustler Joe Rearden has been living in your house for the last several days. He must be powerful important to you to lie and kill for him. The only kinfolk I figure would go that far would be someone's ma or pa."

She didn't reply.

Aaron Smith spoke up. "Your Honor. Just by looking at this poor woman, you can see she had nothing to do with Wiley Bledsoe."

Slade continued, his eyes on Constance Young. He cursed himself for his next words, but he had no choice. "Mrs. Young, I like Joe. We were friends. He told me once that he wanted to buy a small spread up in Wyoming or Montana for him and his ma. I reckon that's a fine idea, but he's hurt real bad right now, and I figure he'd like to have his ma with him."

The apathy disappeared from Constance Young's face as she looked up into Slade's eyes. Her own eyes asked the question. Slade nodded. "He was shot by Kansas Jack. He's over at Caleb Webb's."

"Bad?" She whispered hoarsely.

The young half-breed nodded. "Yes."

With a sharp cry of anguish, she leaped to her feet and, before anyone could stop her, rushed from the building.

CHAPTER
TWENTY-EIGHT

Judge Mayhall's voice boomed above the surprised mutters of the crowd. "Bring that woman back here."

Slade spoke up. "She's not going anywhere, Judge. Only to her son. She'll be there when you want her."

The judge considered Slade's words for a moment, then he nodded.

Later that afternoon, Slade looked down from his pony at Joseph Ware as the blacksmith said, "At least, wait until morning. It'll be dark in a couple hours."

Jake Slade grinned crookedly at the craggy-faced man. "No offense intended, Joseph. But Bent and I would feel a lot more comfortable under the stars than around here."

Bent laughed. "You can say that again." He patted his expanded belly. " 'Course, there are a few things I'll miss."

They all laughed.

Slade tugged on the reins and the Indian pony backed away from the hitching rail. "A favor, Joseph, if you don't mind."

The big blacksmith nodded vigorously. "Name it."

"That girl with the Webbs — Sarah Cook. When I get back to Arizona, I'll send you some money for her with one of our drivers. I'd appreciate you getting it to her. I'd hate for her to end up with the same kind of problems plaguing Miss Young."

Joseph Ware extended his meaty hand. "Don't you worry none, Jake. Mrs. Ware and me'll take care of Sarah, and do all we can for Constance Young, too."

Slade nodded. "Young Joe Rearden. He done some wrong, but he's worth saving."

Ware agreed. "I'll help him all I can, Slade."

"You're a good man, Joseph."

"You, too, Jake." The burly blacksmith hesitated, then looked up into the young half-breed's gray eyes. "You ever coming back this way, Jake?"

Slade studied the older man, and with a wry grin, shook his head. "I reckon not, Joseph." He glanced around the small village. With a rueful chuckle, he added, "Once is enough."

With a click on his tongue and a gentle tug on the reins, Slade turned his pony to the west. Instinctively, his gray eyes scanned the horizon, and for a moment, in his mind's eye, he spotted a dark figure silhouetted against the setting sun.

He drew a deep breath and closed his eyes. When he opened them, the figure had vanished. The young half-breed grimaced at the pain filling his chest, replaced slowly by a growing rage of a fierce loyalty surging through his veins.

Nana was dead. The Indian in Slade knew what was expected of him. He was to avenge his brother's death on the Utes, then bury Nana in the way of the Apache, or die in the effort.

Two hours later as the moon crept over the horizon, Bent and Jake made camp on the rim overlooking the Canadian River Valley. After they crawled into their soogans, Bent gestured upriver. "I reckon old Bill Harnden and you will hafta settle for a station at the other crossing we found. It'll be a damn sight better than back there with Aaron Smith and his bunch."

Slade grinned at his old friend. With a mischievous gleam in his eyes, he replied, "I don't know, Bent. I figure Bill would want us to go back and promise Aaron Smith that if he'd let us in, you'd be the one to stay there and run the relay station."

Bent shot Slade a withering look. "Bull. You and that damned Bill Harnden can go busted as a two-year-old bronc in a rodeo before you'll ever get me back down there in that valley."

The young half-breed laughed. He lay back and stared at the glittering stars overhead. From deep in the night, he heard the call of a bird. He would have sworn it was a whippoorwill, but there were no whippoorwills this time of year. They were gone, just as Nana was gone.

Come spring, the whippoorwill would return, but Nana was never to return.

Slade stared at the three twinkling stars that made up the tail of the great bear, what the white men called the Big Dipper. His eyes focused on the first star, and he whispered in a choked voice, "I'll see you again, brother. And we'll ride and hunt like we did when we were kids." He bit at his bottom lip, and tears filled his eyes.

We hope you have enjoyed this Large Print book. Other Thorndike, Wheeler, and Chivers Press Large Print books are available at your library or directly from the publishers.

For information about current and upcoming titles, please call or write, without obligation, to:

Publisher
Thorndike Press
295 Kennedy Memorial Drive
Waterville, ME 04901
Tel. (800) 223-1244

or visit our Web site at:

www.gale.com/thorndike
www.gale.com/wheeler

OR

Chivers Large Print
published by BBC Audiobooks Ltd
St James House, The Square
Lower Bristol Road
Bath BA2 3SB
England
Tel. +44(0) 800 136919
email: bbcaudiobooks@bbc.co.uk
www.bbcaudiobooks.co.uk

All our Large Print titles are designed for easy reading, and all our books are made to last.